SCAREDY CAT

PANDORA CRESS

First edition: October 2024

Interior Formatting: EJL Editing

Cover Design: @FromAshes.ToPages

Interior Design - Plot Twisted Book Designs

Page Design Model - @TheMaskedMan96

Author's Note

I wrote Scaredy Cat on a whim when I was stuck in bed with the flu. It was a nice mix of my nightmares and imagination fueled by NyQuil, and when I read through my first draft, I thought this would never see the light of day. But, somehow I was able to make sense within the pages and my characters started running the show which has led us here - to an ebook, paperback and audiobook. I don't know how I got so lucky, but I am forever grateful to those that helped me make it happen.

Before we continue, I must warn you that Scaredy Cat is an unhinged tale of dark romance, soul-bargaining, stalking and murder over the course of one fateful Halloween with a touch of the supernatural. Some scenes and actions between the main characters may be disturbing. If you like your books with a healthy dose of trigger warnings and like to be surprised, you can now skip ahead. For those who would like to know what you're getting yourselves into, readers should be aware that this book contains the following.

Invasion of Privacy

Manipulation

Mentions of Drug Use

Age Gap (Centuries)
Occult Activity
Unknown Voyeurism
Kidnapping
Sacrificial Murder
Dubious and Non-Consent
Blood Play
Knife Play
Fear Play
Anal Play
Pain Play
Primal Play
Mask Play
Forced Orgasms
Use of Sex Toys
Breath Play
Leash Play
Choking
Inappropriate Use of a Demon Tail
Double Penetration.

I would like to give you a chance to turn back at this point if anything mentioned upsets you. This book is meant to be a fast-paced, exciting read but you are meant to feel disoriented alongside our female lead which can cause feelings of panic. The activities involved in this story are fueled by supernatural instincts, much like that of a drug, and therefore may cause distress as to how far our characters are willing to go.

SCAREDY CAT PLAYLIST

SHAKE YOUR KITTY

LADY GAGA 3:45

THE OTHERSIDE
JAKE DANIELS

KILLER
VALERIE BROUSSARD

SOMEBODYS WATCHING ME
ROCKWELL

STRAIGHT TO HELL
LVCRFT / SABRINA SPELLMAN

RITUALS
JIOVANNI DANIEL

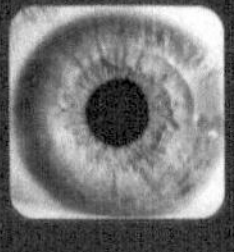
DEVIL I KNOW
ALLIE X

SCAREDY CATTY
CJBEARDS

DARKSIDE
NEONI

MOTHERLAND
REACH

HOW VILLIANS ARE MADE
MADELAN DUKE

BLACK MAGIC WOMAN
VCTRYS

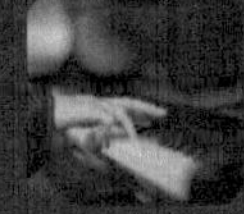
LOOK WHAT YOU MADE ME DO
TAYLOR SWIFT

Dedication

To all the girls who wish they had magic powers,
Maybe you just haven't been fucked hard enough by a
demon yet.

For the rest of you,
Grab your candy corn and vibrator.
Halloween isn't finished, but I hope you do.

Chapter 1
Zach

I reclined in my seat, the heat from my steaming coffee sending a pleasant shiver through me as I took my first sip. Stacey's laughter brought my gaze to her as I took in the easy way she sat in the small coffee shop. It was a soft, melodic sound that drew me in and even I couldn't discern if it was from the hold she had over me or just something inherently...her. She sat with two friends, a couple of striking girls, all blonde-haired and sweet. Yet Stacey, sporting that daring crimson stripe that framed her face against her dark locks, appeared to outshine the others.

"C'mon, Stacey! It's Halloween! You have to go to the party!" One of her friends pouted, her perfectly styled hair cascading over her shoulders.

Stacey shook her head, a playful grin dancing on her red lips. "Sorry, Jenna. I can't promise anything. Matt and I might have something more... exciting to do tonight."

The other girls leaned in, intrigued.

"What do you mean?" her other friend asked, her brows furrowed in confusion.

"Okay, hear me out," Stacey said as her voice dropped to a low whisper. "I've always wanted to role-play being chased and kidnapped. Just think about it—creepy vibes, dark corners, all the danger. And the getting caught part?" Stacey winked and the girls laughed. "Haven't you roleplayed before, Mia?"

Mia's baby blue eyes widened. "Yes. In bed. *On a Wednesday.* With someone I trusted. Not someone I picked up in a bar who is barely a boyfriend." Mia rubbed her temples before she looked at Stacey again and I hid my smile behind my cup as I continued to listen. "Kidnapped? Seriously? You want to play that on Halloween?"

"Why not? It's the perfect night for it." Stacey leaned forward, completely disregarding Mia's dig. "I've got a new boyfriend who's not opposed to it. We can set the whole scene. He also didn't look at me like I was demented like my exes when I brought it up to him."

I sipped my coffee, listening intently. Stacey's energy radiated off her, and it wasn't just from the coffee she was drinking. She was genuinely getting off on the idea. She was so giddy that she completely ignored her friends and their hesitancy toward it. Which was hard to do, considering the girls exchanged glances that practically shouted how bad of an idea they thought it was.

"That's because he's on so many drugs he probably doesn't even know what you were talking about," Jenna said as she rolled her eyes, her tone half-teasing.

"Yeah, and what if he takes it too far?" Mia's concern laced her words. "You know how guys can be. You want to be careful."

Stacey waved her hand dismissively. "It'll be fine. We'll set boundaries. It'll just be a fun little game." She leaned back, a satisfied smirk on her lips. "Besides, what's the worst that could happen?"

The girls really did have a point. This was not a night to be playing around unless you wanted to find yourself in some pretty nasty trouble.

Poor thing had no idea what I had in store for her.

I shifted in my seat, and looked up to find one of the server's standing beside my table asking if I needed anything. I shook my head, not entirely able to keep my attention off of my beautiful prey. She had a way of pulling people in, making them want to be near her. It's something that came natural to people like Stacey. She was a supernatural magnet, and she was about to find out that she'd pulled me right to her.

The idea of her playing the helpless victim resonated in my mind, swirling like the steam rising from my cup of coffee. It was the perfect opportunity to reel her in, honestly. I needed to be part of her world, even if just for a moment if my plan was going to work.

I needed to catch her off-guard if I was going to sweep her off her feet. All I had to do was get close enough to snag her phone.

With that, I could slip into her life like she'd slipped into my mind.

As her group began to rise, I noticed the way she tucked her phone into her purse, her movements slow and confident. My heart raced and I could feel it pounding inside my chest.

God, I missed this feeling.

Being dead was such a bitch.

I stood, shoving my sheets of music I'd been working on into a haphazard pile. It was something I was known for in a past life that was so long ago, I could barely remember. To think I had sold my soul centuries ago to be known as the best pianist of the time only to contract the plague was the devil's joke, I'm sure. I thought I would finally have it all only to have it stripped from me. After the devil made me into this thing, this slave to him, I went a little insane getting used to my newly forged path as a demon. The only consolation was having a taste of life once a year to again be torn back to the fiery home I now had.

The devil had jokes, but I would have the last laugh this year.

I stepped into her path, the world narrowing to just the two of us.

"Oops! Sorry!" I bumped into her, feigning surprise as her purse tipped, spilling its contents onto the cherry-wood floor around us. My pages of music fluttered about like oversized confetti and she looked around hastily at the scene we'd caused.

Stacey bent down, a frown momentarily flickering across her face before she flashed a quick smile. "No worries! It was just an accident."

"Let me help you." I said as I knelt, my fingers brushing against her plain black iphone as I gathered the scattered items. I could feel her gaze lingering on me, curiosity mixed with a hint of flirtation.

"Wow, you write songs," Stacey remarked, picking up a crumpled drawing of the tire.

"Just something to pass the time." I shrugged, forcing a casual tone. "I tend to get inspired by beautiful things."

Stacey's friends giggled behind her, a lightness in the air that made my heart thump louder. Fuck, this human body felt good. The adrenaline. I missed it so fucking much.

A blush rose to Stacey's cheeks and she looked so innocent across from me in that ridiculous bat sweatshirt and leggings. Her friends were wearing similar attire now that I took a moment to take them in, casual with a hint of the holiday on display.

I slid her phone into my pocket, the weight of it a comforting promise of the plans I had made moments ago.

"Here, let me get that for you. I'm Zach," I said as I smiled and stood to offer her the remnants of her scattered purse.

"Stacey," she said as she pointed to herself before grabbing her things. "Thanks! I really appreciate it."

She beamed at me and the warmth of her smile ignited something within me. Something I was trying to keep in check to the best of my devilish abilities.

I couldn't take my eyes off her. I held her gaze, holding my breath even as her friends called for her to hurry up.

"I should get going," she said, glancing over her shoulder. "But maybe I'll see you around?"

Her voice lilted at the end, turning her statement into a question. I grinned.

"I'd like that." I winked and folded my arms across my chest where I held my papers to me. I wanted to show off how nice this body was for her. I'd been very selective coming back this time if I was to keep this form for awhile and the way Stacey was looking at how my biceps stretched the sleeves of my black button-up, I think I picked a winner.

A pretty blush rose on Stacey's cheeks once more as she tore her gaze from the tattoos on my neck.

"Happy Halloween." She said and offered me a coy smile before turning to leave, her hips swaying as she walked away.

I watched her go, desire and anticipation churning within me. Soon, very soon, she would be mine. For now, I had to bide my time and wait for the perfect opportunity to strike.

Stacey looked back at me once more as she reached the café door, giving a little wave before disappearing outside. I raised my hand in return, already imagining what it would feel like to have these fingers wrapped around that slender neck of hers.

Yes, she was the one. My perfect, pretty little prey for this year's Halloween ritual. I licked my lips in anticipation, barely able to contain my true nature.

Just a little longer...

And then her soul would set me free.

Chapter 2
Stacey

I sat cross-legged on the plush carpet of my bedroom, surrounded by piles of hastily gathered outfits and discarded costume pieces. My estate loomed around me, grand and beautiful, with high ceilings and intricate moldings. All white on white because who can be posh anymore without completely getting rid of any semblance of personality. I often rolled my eyes at the thought of how much money my parents had spent on this place. It was just a house, after all, but other than me, their money was the most important thing to them and they liked to spend it.

I still had hopes of getting to the party later so I wanted to be prepared.

A sparkly vampire cape? Too blah. A fairy with wings? It would be too cold. I rifled through a box of accessories, tossing aside scraps of glitter and sequins. Halloween was my favorite holiday, and I always dressed up. Usually an elaborate idea I would work on for months. But with the hope of being chased and kidnapped at some point tonight, I wanted to be relatively comfortable.

I leaned back against the white velvet bench that was at the foot of my matching four-poster bed, pondering my options. Maybe I could do something simple, something playful. I did want to play, after all.

Grabbing a pair of cat ears from the pile, I laughed at the idea. A classic, but who was I to resist? I plucked a black eyeliner from my vanity and started drawing whiskers on my face, giggling at my reflection.

"Perfect," I murmured, admiring my impromptu feline transformation in the mirror. I had thrown on a long-sleeved black sweater over my black bra and opted for no panties, finishing the look with a short black skirt and fishnet stockings. I grabbed my black pair of Doc Martens and I was complete. I might not be going all out, but at least I was festive. And Matt *was* a bit of a dog, so this was perfect.

With a satisfied look on my face that would mirror the best of any cat I had seen, I headed to the kitchen to grab a snack before I called Matt to see what time we were meeting up. My black purse sat starkly on the marble countertop, the only thing of color in this room as well. I reached for it and peered inside. And found...no phone.

No phone.

No phone?

Panic prickled at my skin as I tore through my purse and ran back to rummage through my room on the off chance I had brought it in there with me when I got home.

"Where is it?" I muttered, my heart racing. I couldn't be without my phone, not tonight. Tonight was supposed to be the night things finally worked out for me. I was desperate to have my first orgasm and after twenty six years, I fucking deserved one.

Just as the dread began to settle in, the house phone rang. I stared at it, puzzled. The landline? No one ever called it, except my parents but they were on vacation until Thanksgiving and there was no way they'd interrupt their time sightseeing Greece to check on me. I hesitated before walking over to it, glancing back at my purse, hoping my phone would magically appear.

"Hello?" I picked up the receiver, a knot of anxiety tightening in my stomach. I was a woman alone on Halloween in this giant manor after all.

"Stacey?"

I recognized the voice from this morning instantly. "Zach?"

"Yeah, hey! Your phone ended up in my things by accident."

"Accident?"

"I tried calling some of what I assumed were your friends, but no one picked up. I figured I'd try the number listed as 'Home' on the off chance you still had a landline."

My heart thudded. "So, you have my phone?"

"Yeah, I'd love to give it back. I can wait for you at the café."

I took a deep breath, relief and a little bit of excitement washing over me at the chance to see this man again. "Okay, I'll be there."

"Looking forward to it."

I hung up, feeling a little better and totally weirded out at the same time.. A stranger had my phone. Well, not a stranger *exactly.* Zach had it. Zach had my phone and my non-existent panties in a twist and I didn't even know him.

But I had to get it back if I was going to go through with my plans tonight. I didn't have Matt's number memorized since we'd only just started dating a couple weeks ago. Or rather, sleeping together. He didn't take me on dates outside of his bedroom which was why I was so excited about tonight.

I set the receiver down, unease curling in my stomach.

Zach seemed like an okay guy, but the thought of him rifling through my stuff felt invasive. My phone held more than just contacts; it stored my life—photos, messages, secrets. Nudes.

Fuck. I ran my fingers through my hair and then cursed again as the cat ears topped off my head. I picked them off the ground and put them back in place before taking a breath, trying to shake off the creeping anxiety.

I grabbed my keys and dashed out the door, locking it behind me. The cool evening air hit my face, and I hurried to my car before making the short drive down the street toward the café. Street lights flickered on, casting long shadows across the road as I drove in silence. I couldn't shake the feeling that something was off and my instincts were usually spot on. Each stop light I came to immediately turned green and I clapped my hands once, laughing at my luck. I loved when that happened when I was in a hurry, it was such an awesome coincidence.

The café came into view, its warm glow spilling out onto the sidewalk. There were several jack-o-lanterns placed in front of the steps now as the sun was going down and I grinned at them as I pushed the door open, the bell jingling overhead. The familiar aroma of coffee and baked goods wrapped around me and I instantly felt more at ease in my favorite place. But the comfort faded as I spotted Zach at a corner table, tapping his fingers against the wooden surface. He looked up, a smirk spreading across his face.

"Over here!" he called, waving me over.

I forced a smile, my nerves tightening again as I approached. "So, you really had my phone, huh?"

"Yeah, sorry about that. I must have thought it was mine at first." He slid my phone across the table. "I was about to just look at your contact information to find where you lived and bring it back to you.

My stomach flipped but then I remembered, "I don't keep my address stored in there."

"Probably a safe bet. You never know who can get a hold of personal information and use it against you." Zach paused to wink at me and *why did that send a rush between my thighs*? We were talking about my safety—lack thereof in a worst case scenario and I was getting wet? "Figured I'd call the one that said 'Home' instead."

"Right." I picked up the phone, relieved but still unsettled with both him and my impure thoughts. "Thanks, I guess."

Zach leaned back, a playful spark in his eyes. "You should've heard your voice when I told you I'd found it. You were ready to freak out."

"Yeah, well..." I trailed off, unsure how to express the feeling of violation. It wasn't just about the phone. "It's just weird, you know? Having someone else go through your stuff."

He nodded, his expression shifting to something more serious. "I get it. I didn't mean to make you uncomfortable."

I sighed, staring down at my phone, the weight of it reminding me that I should look through my messages to see if Matt had texted anything. Nothing. "It's fine."

"Want to grab a drink?" He offered, trying to lighten the mood.

"Sure, but I think I need something stronger than coffee," I muttered as I slipped my phone into the pocket of my skirt. So much for Matt.

"Now you're talking."

As he stood and went to open the door for me, I caught a glimpse of my reflection in the café's window. The cat ears perched atop my head felt ridiculous, and the whiskers I'd drawn seemed less fun now as I stood beside this handsome stranger. We were both dressed in all black and honestly looked like a striking couple having a date on Halloween. I scolded myself in my mind as I thought back to Matt. I had been with a few other guys before Matt but hadn't felt much of a spark with any of them. I figured it was because they were presented to me like gifts from my family and friends of theirs. They'd grown up like me

- privileged and spoiled. But where I longed for the next exciting thing to happen, they were utterly boring. And much worse was that none of them had been able to get me off.

Not once.

I'd played with myself on and off for years and it felt good but I hadn't been able to get past that "peak" everyone talks about. My mom even paid for a sex therapist when I finished college. Having homework that required "private time" with yourself was beyond awkward and in fact made any progress I was making completely tank.

I asked Matt out on purpose when I met him at a bar a few weeks ago. I could tell he wasn't into anything serious and was just looking for some fun. My thought process was that maybe I had been dating guys that were too uptight. Maybe I needed one that had less inhibitions and had more grit to him. Yeah, he had a drug problem but he had a dirty mouth and got me close a couple times in the back seat of his car.

And here I was, dressed as a cat with the most handsome man I'd ever laid eyes on about to get a drink.

What a night this was turning out to be.

Zach held the door open, and I stepped out into the brisk October chill. The atmosphere crackled with excitement, with laughter flowing from nearby houses and businesses in our charming little town. He fell into step beside me, the weight of the evening's earlier awkwardness dissipating as we walked and took in the people celebrating around us. He was still dressed in all black. Black jeans with his black button-up, yet his sleeves were rolled to his elbows now showing off even more artwork etched into his tan skin.

"Check out the costumes," he said, nodding at a group of witches cackling outside a bar, their pointed hats bobbing as they laughed. "Looks like the whole town came out to play."

I glanced around, and smiled. "Yeah, it's pretty wild." My eyes landed on a couple dressed as superheroes, their capes flapping in the breeze.

Zach led me down the street, past a gaudy display of flashing lights. The bar loomed ahead, its entrance crowded with costumed patrons. A banner overhead proclaimed, "Spooktacular Night!"

"Let's grab that drink," he suggested, pushing through the throng of people.

Inside, the atmosphere blared with drunk voices and music. We squeezed up to the bar, the wooden surface sticky under my fingers. I grimaced as I wiped my hands on my skirt and then placed my purse on the back of the bar stool as I sat down and scanned the drink menu, but my mind was elsewhere.

"What's your poison?" Zach asked, his brow raised.

"Something strong and fruity," I replied, trying to shake off the tension creeping back in. "I need a distraction."

He ordered us both cocktails while I pulled out my phone, hoping to text Matt. I'd left him a message earlier today before I lost my phone, but he hadn't replied. I frowned at the screen, my fingers hovering over the keyboard.

"Everything okay?" Zach leaned in, watching me.

"Just trying to reach my boyfriend," I mumbled, tapping the screen again. "He's being weird about texting back. He didn't happen to message me when you had my phone, did he?"

"Sorry, no. Maybe he's busy with his own Halloween plans," Zach offered, though his tone seemed like he was quite happy about that idea.

I shrugged, trying to ignore the nagging feeling in my gut.

Just as our drinks arrived, Zach excused himself. "I'll be right back," he said, weaving through the crowd toward the restroom, the eyes of the women in the bar following him. I couldn't blame them since I couldn't help myself as I stared after him, too. He was very tall, at least 6'5 and had dark hair like mine though obviously shorter. His black jeans hugged his muscular thighs and a backside that should have been in a Calvin Klein commercial. I was just taking in how his back flexed through his black Henley as he pushed open the bathroom door at the back of the bar when someone bumped my stool.

I blushed and took a sip of my drink, the sweetness washing over me, and tried texting Matt again. Still no response. I chewed my lip, glancing around the bar. The costumed crowd laughed and danced, oblivious to my relationship problems.

What does a girl have to do to find a guy who is into kinky shit?

I took a chance on Matt specifically because he wasn't necessarily the best character. My friends couldn't believe it when I brought him home from the bar. They were used to me dating upstanding men from society. Ones my parents hand-picked me. Ones that had money and no personality.

Matt was a rockstar wanna-be druggie who didn't treat me like a lady. He didn't treat me like anything at all really, except a decent lay every now and then which was more than I was getting with the guys at my parent's country club. I had been so close to an orgasm the last time because he got rough with me and my body loved it. I assumed I could work out *some* of these sexual fantasies with him and get them out of my system, FINALLY get to that point in my sexual career and move on. But the bastard seemed to have partied too hard tonight.

Then, finally, my phone buzzed. I quickly unlocked it, my eyes taking in the text.

Meet me at the entrance to the Loden Woods. Hope you wore sneakers. I'm about to make all your fantasies come to life.

My eyes widened as I stared at the screen.

What? So he was going to go through with this?

I glanced around me and stared back at my phone, a mix of anticipation and excitement mixing with the alcohol.

I tucked my phone into my purse just as Zach emerged from the bathroom, his thick dark hair falling slightly over his forehead, a smile dancing on his lips. God, he was too sexy for this earth, I swear. And charming. He obviously came from money, too, which made him almost too good to be true with my former experiences.

I raised my glass to my mouth, taking a hasty sip and the DJ started playing *Somebody's Watching Me* by Rockwell.

Perfect. Let's add to my paranoia.

Zach slid onto the bar stool next to me, his gaze settling on my face with an intensity that made my heart flutter. He leaned closer, resting his arms on the counter. "You okay?"

"Yeah, just thirsty," I said as I took another drink and then dropped my hands in my lap to play with the hem of my skirt. What was it about this guy? He made me feel like a teenager again, not a woman in her mid-twenties who'd never gotten off in her life. I think that was the problem. He looked like he could do it.

He even looked like he wanted to.

"Right." He raised an eyebrow, his voice teasing. "Thirsty or nervous?"

I bounced my leg under the table, the rhythm betraying me. I tried to play it cool, but every time he looked at me, my body reacted.

Zach reached out and grabbed my thigh, his fingers warm against my skin even through the fishnet fabric that clung to them. I was startled, but tried to hide it.

"You're really jittery," he said, studying me.

I laughed quickly, brushing it off. "I had too much caffeine today, that's all."

"Caffeine?" His tone suggested he wasn't buying it. "You sure that's all?"

The warmth of his hand lingered on my leg, and I fought to suppress a moan. "Yeah, just the excitement of Halloween."

"You're excited, huh?" He leaned back, a knowing smile on his face. His eyes dropped to my chest and I could feel my nipples harden. I hoped he couldn't tell through my sweater. "I guess I can see that." *Shit.*

I tried to focus on my drink, but the way his fingers pressed against my thigh sent me spiraling. "You're just making me think about my costume," I said, forcing a laugh that didn't quite match the tension in the air. I needed to change the subject and fast.

"Which is?" he prompted, a glint in his bright green eyes.

"Um, just a cat obviously," I said, shrugging and pointing to the ears. "Nothing too wild."

Zach smirked, and his grip moved another inch higher on my thigh. "I guess it does seem a little tame for a night like this."

I bit my lip, trying to hide the smile threatening to break free. "Maybe I'm just trying to keep it low-key tonight."

"Low-key doesn't look like that." His thumb brushed against my inner thigh, and my breath caught.

My heart raced as I glanced away, the atmosphere affecting me almost as much as the drink I had in my hand. I couldn't tell if it was the drink or him, but my nerves danced, a tightrope walk between desire and dread because why was I still here? With a strange man at a bar and not with my boyfriend?

Zach seemed to sense me stiffen and moved his hand off my thigh to flick at the cat ears on top of my head. I crossed my legs, hoping to shake off the heat radiating from where his hand had lingered. The shift brought some relief, but the tension between us only seemed to thicken, like an invisible thread pulling tighter and tighter and -

"So, I really need to meet up with Matt soon," I said, making myself get the words out, trying to divert my mind from the warmth of his touch.

Zach just grinned, taking me in with that calm, steady gaze. "You guys have special plans before the party?"

"Uh, yeah. Something like that," I replied, a slight tremor in my voice. "I just want to make sure we're on the same page." Wait. Hold on. "How do you know about the party?"

He chuckled softly, leaning back as he looked at his drink, something blue and fruity because there was an orange and cherries on top. I just noticed how silly it looked to see such a towering specimen of a man drinking something so girly. "Actually, your friends texted you about it earlier tonight. I happened to see the notifications on your phone."

"Great. I thought you hadn't gone through my phone."

"Relax, it's not a big deal," Zach said, but I wasn't convinced. I don't care how hot this guy was, I couldn't help but feel like he'd gone through those nudes I was worried about. Mia keeps scolding me about putting a lock on my phone and now I realize I should have listened to her.

I glanced at my drink, feeling the weight of the conversation press down on me. "I should probably pay for this."

He grabbed my hand, preventing me from paying with the $20 bill I'd just pulled from my wallet. "Let me get this," he insisted.

I nodded and put my things back in my purse and mumbled a 'thank you' as I tried to look at anywhere else in the bar that wasn't his face. He didn't seem to like that and grasped my chin to turn my gaze back to his.

"Maybe I'll go to that party of yours. It would be a shame to see such a beautiful pussy go alone." He leaned closer, the moment stretching between us, charged with unspoken words.

I opened my mouth to respond, but my heart raced, caught in the web of his filthy words and the danger that radiated off him.

He looked like he was about to eat me.

And I was about to let him.

Without another word, I pulled away from him and bolted from the bar.

Chapter 3
Zach

I watched her leave, my eyes tracing every curve of her body. The way her hips swayed as she walked away, the gentle bounce of her hair - it was fucking mesmerizing. My throat went dry, and I couldn't shake the heat from where my hand had touched her thigh.

Her scent still hung in the air, a mix of vanilla and clove and something uniquely her. I closed my eyes, savoring it, committing it to memory. The sound of her nervous laughter echoed in my mind, and I found myself grinning at the thought of how adorable she looked when flustered.

Replaying our conversation in my head, I focused on the way my name sounded on her lips. There was something about the way she said it, a hint of breathlessness that sent blood straight to my cock. And those lips - so soft, so inviting. I couldn't stop thinking about how they'd feel against my skin.

The phone in my pocket buzzed, snapping me out of my reverie. I glanced down, seeing Stacey's name flash across the screen. A message popped up:

> **Matt? Are you sure I'm supposed to meet you at the woods?**

My grin widened. Everything was falling into place. I quickly typed back a simple **"yes"** in response. Another message came through almost immediately.

> I thought the way you were ignoring me earlier meant you weren't into it. I know it was a weird ask and we haven't been dating very long. We don't need to do this unless you're sure.

I chuckled softly to myself. If only she knew what was really going on. I didn't respond, letting her fret about our encounter. My mind drifted back to the way she looked in that cat costume. Something so childish looked so decadent on her that it should have been a sin. In fact, from where I came from I'm sure that it was.

I sighed as I stood up, leaving some cash on the bar for our drinks. As I walked out of the bar, I couldn't help how exhilarated I felt this Halloween. Tonight was going to be unforgettable. And that kitty. That pussy. Was finally about to be mine.

There were pumpkins lining the streets, casting a warm glow on the pavement. My pulse quickened as I rounded the corner, eager to see my ride. There it was, gleaming under the soft light of a vintage-looking streetlamp—my black 1955 Mercedes GullWing 300SL. A handful of people stood nearby, their eyes wide, mouths agape, like kids in a candy store. The fuckers were practically drooling and I couldn't help but smirk at the sight.

"Damn, man, look at that!" one guy exclaimed, nudging his buddy.

"Is that even real?" the other replied, leaning closer, eyes scanning the curves of the car.

I checked my watch. 6:19 P.M. Cutting it close, but I still had several hours before midnight.

I took a moment to soak it all in, the attention, the envy. Maybe I should've gone with something a little more under the radar, but I literally sold my soul for luxuries like this. No point in holding back now.

I approached the car, feeling the cool metal beneath my fingertips. The door opened upwards, a sleek arc toward the sky. The onlookers gasped, and I couldn't stop a laugh as I slid into the driver's seat, the leather hugging me like an old friend.

"Holy shit, you own this?" one of the guys asked, stepping closer, clearly impressed.

"Yeah, it's mine," I said, a grin stretching across my face. I cranked the ignition, the engine roared to life, echoing through the quiet street.

"Man, I've never seen one up close," the guy continued, eyes wide with awe.

I shrugged, feigning nonchalance. "Just a little something I picked up."

I checked my watch, a sleek black Rolex that matched the car's glossy exterior. Time slipped through my fingers on these special Halloween nights, but I had to make sure every second counted. Another expensive purchase for today, but it felt good on my wrist, the weight reminding me of all the pain and suffering that got me here.

I glanced into the back seat, heart racing a little. The costume I had picked up earlier lay there, neatly folded beside my Spirit Halloween bag. My dick twitched as I spotted the mask perched on top. It stared back at me, a simple skull mask but in red. A classic, just like her outfit.

Perfect for the night ahead.

I revved the engine again, the roar vibrating through my bones. A quick glance around revealed a few lingering admirers, which I have to say did wonders for my ego. I shifted into gear and tore down the street, and the world blurred by as I accelerated, the thrill of speed coursing through me. I have to admit, driving was my favorite part of this future I could have missed out on. My soul was taken in 1798 so I had acclimated to multiple changes in that timeframe. The drugs, music and sex got better over time, though.

As I turned onto the winding road leading to the woods, the trees closed in around me, shadows dancing in the headlights. Tonight, everything felt right. I could already picture Stacey's face when she saw me in the costume, the playful banter that would follow. The moans. The shock when she realized she'd been completely and thoroughly taken advantage of. I looked in the rearview mirror, catching a glimpse of the mask. It seemed to grin back at me, almost as if it understood all my fucked up plans.

"Just a little more fun, just a little longer," I muttered to myself, the words barely escaping my lips.

I pressed the gas pedal harder, the engine growling beneath me. The trees blurred into streaks of brown and orange as I drove, but my thoughts lingered on Stacey. Every year, I played this game—dancing through this special annual affair, searching for a soul so perfectly made for my taking. The soul that would bind to mine and allow me to stay here and enjoy these mortal spoils. Halloween had become my one chance to walk amongst the living, a single day where I could feel human again. I knew that if I could figure out how to stay, even for just one lifetime it would piss the devil off that his contracted demon had found a loophole. I'd give up most of my powers, but after all these years I still hadn't found anyone worth the trade.

Until now.

Stacey could feel it, too. I know she could. She had this way of looking at me, like I mattered, and that was rare. I'd watched her with cautious hope, waiting for the moment I could let my guard down. It took every ounce of patience to keep from rushing in and just tossing her in my trunk when I felt her skin through those stockings.

I navigated the twists of the road, realizing I was almost where I needed to be. The memories of her playful teasing took over my thoughts. I had actually found her last year, with only an hour to spare before my time amongst the living was up. But I had smelled her and I knew.

I knew I had finally found one. A *real* one.

"Are you sure you're not secretly a superhero?" she had asked, that sexy grin lighting up her eyes. She was busy looking at the car I chose to drive around last year. A black

2015 SLS AMG. Always black. A hard color to let go of when you've spent over 200 years in the shadows of hell.

"Maybe I am," I'd shot back, my heart racing. "Or maybe I just drive cool cars to impress pretty things like you."

She had blushed and hugged her arms around her mid-section to shield herself from the night air as she waited outside the café for her friends to join her. The three of them were dressed like the Sanderson sisters from Hocus Pocus and their wigs were impressive to say the least. She kept glancing back toward the cafe windows, willing her friends to come out.

"Is it working?" I asked when she didn't respond.

"Is what working?"

"Are you impressed?" I laughed and leaned against the hood of the car, crossing my arms over my chest.

She tossed her blonde plastic locks over her shoulder and stood straighter.

"I'd be more impressed if you showed me you knew how to drive it."

"Would you like to go for a ride?" My tone suggested more than just driving around for a few blocks.

Her mouth opened to respond as her friends finally stepped out behind her. The tension was palpable but the moment was gone as quickly as it came. I gave her a wink and got into the car without another word and watched her walk off down the street with her friends.

And now, a year later, I was right where I wanted to be. I'd upgraded and found an extremely handsome young man with a chiseled body, a splattering of tattoos and dark hair. He had my eyes, though. The one thing that I had any control over when it comes to this sort of thing. I have to say, the pierced dick was definitely something I wasn't prepared for, but I could get used to it.

The man had no living family or kin, a loner. He'd been in a motorcycle accident and declared brain dead. Those are the easy contracts, they don't know how to do much of anything so getting them to agree to take their soul is a piece of cake.

Ohhh, cake. I forgot about cake. I hadn't eaten any this year and needed to make a note to do so.

I had never believed I'd get this moment after all these years of searching. Pure-blooded witches were almost eradicated after that terrible little shitshow in Salem some years back.

The weight of the red skull mask in the back seat felt heavier now. I hadn't thought of anything else besides this girl for the last 365 days. Stacey had opened a door I thought was forever locked, and I longed to step through it, to be real, to be alive. Officially.

As I approached the woods, my heart thudded in my chest.

My borrowed human heart.

What if tonight changed everything?

What if I could finally be human, if only for one lifetime?

What if...

I tightened my grip on the wheel.

Chapter 4
Stacey

6:49 P.M.
Halloween

I felt absolutely ridiculous standing at the entrance of the woods. The trees towered above me like giants, their gnarled branches reaching out, casting long shadows across the ground. I wasn't that easy to scare, but the night was playing tricks on my sight and I couldn't help but want to just get back in my car and leave. I tugged at the hem of my skirt, feeling the scratchy fabric of the fishnets dig into my skin under it. The cat ears perched on my head felt more like a costume malfunction than a clever accessory standing out here by myself.

A cold gust of wind rustled the leaves, sending the cold down my spine. I shifted my weight between my feet, keeping my body moving so I wouldn't start shivering. My eyes trailed back toward the main road, the distant sound of laughter and chatter echoing in the night in the town just a few blocks away. Maybe I should have just gone with my friends. I was so desperate to get to this point -

to break through this mental barrier and finally have an orgasm that I was completely talking myself out of being logical. I could be sipping warm beer from a solo cup at Mia's house where it was safe, but instead here I was alone, scared and ready to face the night.

I took a few hesitant steps forward, the path beneath my feet crunching with colorful fallen leaves. The clearing had felt safe, but now the shadows closed in around me, whispering that danger was near. This wasn't how I envisioned the night going. My twisted fantasies had always been a part of me that felt more like a guilty pleasure than reality. I didn't act on them. Until Matt said he was up for it.

"Come on, Stacey," I muttered to myself, shaking my head. "It's just a little fun. This was your idea, after all. Chill the fuck out."

I paused, inhaling the damp, earthy scent of the woods. He must be close and I could feel my heart rate stutter. Maybe this would be my chance to shed the good girl act, to tease the edges of my morals for once without regret.

I glanced back down the path, my heart pounding. "Where are you, Matt?" I whispered into the stillness, my voice barely breaking the silence as it blended in with the sound of the rustling leaves around me.

The woods seemed to hold their breath with me.

Waiting.

I walked a few yards into the wooded area, the moon my only light as I pushed past some low-lying branches. The noise from town faded behind me, swallowed by the thick of the trees. I paused to look into the darkness that surrounded me, but there was nothing.

Then it went so silent. I couldn't hear the sounds of people anymore. The cheerful shouts and music vanished as if the woods absorbed them, leaving only the sound of my breath in my ears. I strained to catch any hint of life—birds, crickets, even the rustle of leaves—but nothing stirred. A knot tightened in my stomach.

No, I couldn't hear anything, but I could *feel.*

I gasped as a chill crawled down my spine, and just as I turned to take a step back, I felt his breath on the back of my shoulder. Warm, almost intimate, and it sent a jolt through me.

"Didn't think you'd actually come out here," the figure murmured, his voice low and teasing.

I spun around, my heart racing. He looked terrifying. Dressed in all black with a black hoodie pulled over his head where a red skeleton mask clung to his face. He turned me back around so I was facing away from him.

"Thought I was gonna be all alone," I shot back, feigning bravado even as my pulse quickened.

"Where's the fun in that?" He stepped closer, the space between us charged. The voice was muffled behind the mask, but it sounded deeper than Matt's usual timbre.

I swallowed hard, and I started trembling almost immediately. I wasn't prepared for how intense this was going to be once I was in the woods with a masked man. My body couldn't decide if it was ready to bolt from fright or melt in a puddle of lust. "This is just a game, right?"

He brought my body to his and it sounded like he was breathing me in, revealing something more dangerous lurking behind his charm. "Let's find out."

The ground scraped against my palms as I landed, the damp earth sinking beneath me. I didn't expect him to be so rough. The shock of him pushing me to the ground held me in place for a moment, breathless and wide-eyed. I stared up at him, that damned mask obscuring his expression, yet I could feel the intensity of his gaze.

"Run," he said, his voice a low rumble that sent a shiver through me.

I scrambled backward, my heart pounding against my ribcage and leaves tangling in my tights.

He tilted his masked face as he took me in and folded his arms across his chest. I might have been reeling from this whole situation but I could swear he looked taller from this angle.

"I'm going to tell you one more time," he growled. "But it's only fair to warn you that you have no chance of escaping me." He took a step forward to bend down toward me, blocking out the light of the moon behind him so all I saw was the shadowed outline of his mask. "You can run all you want, little kitty, but I will catch you. I will have my tongue buried in that pussy. And I will fuck those cat ears right off your pretty little head before this night is over."

Where the fuck did that come from? My legs shook as I found my footing, and before I could process what was happening, I took off into the woods. The branches snagged at my clothes, but I pushed through, driven by adrenaline. He never spoke to me like that before. Never. And I loved it. I was so wet that I could feel the slick cool against the apex of my thighs as I ran with everything I had.

I could hear him behind me, the soft rustle of leaves and the crunch of twigs breaking underfoot. But each time I risked a glance over my shoulder, I found only darkness. Fear twisted in my stomach. He was close, but I couldn't see him.

"Matt?" I called, but the word felt small in the vastness of the woods. No answer came, only the whispers of the wind through the trees.

I focused on my path, dodging low branches and the gnarled roots that threatened to trip me. I tried not to veer too far from the main path because the only thing that scared me more than the man in the woods with me was the thought I could get lost here. The air felt thick, as if the forest itself conspired to trap me. My lungs burned with each breath, but I kept running.

I could hear him trailing me, but there was something so incredibly unsettling about not being able to catch a glimpse of him. I imagined him right behind me, ready to pounce, the thrill of the chase blending with a feeling of excitement that I had never associated with desire like this. Maybe I really was onto something, these darker sexual needs were what it took to truly get me off.

I pushed harder, my heart racing, but the trees seemed to stretch on forever. I had never run like this, never felt so alive and terrified all at once. Then, in a moment of instinct, I ducked behind a thick trunk, pressing myself against the rough bark. My sweater tore near my left shoulder and I cursed before I held my breath. There I sat, hoping to hear him pass by, but all I could hear was the rapid thumping of my heart.

Then, I heard it. A twig snapped, the sound sharp in the stillness. I let out a slow, steady breath, praying I'd blend into the shadows. My fingers dug into the bark, grounding me, but my mind raced with thoughts. What was I doing?

This wasn't a game anymore.

"Stacey," his voice called out, low and teasing, just a breath away from me. "You can't hide that tight little pussy from me forever."

My pulse quickened at his words and my knees knocked together as I brought them up to hug against my chest.

Wait a second, I thought it was the mask making his voice sound different but... That did not sound like Matt. Matt didn't say my name like that.

"I know you're close, Stacey," he continued, and the way he said my name sent a chill down my spine.

Oh.

My.

God.

This wasn't Matt. *Who the fuck IS CHASING ME THROUGH THE WOODS?*

I couldn't let him find me. I couldn't give in. I glanced to my right, looking for a way to escape, but the shadows stretched out like dark tendrils. I needed to move, to run again, but the thought of being caught froze me in place.

Suddenly, a soft rustle came from my left, and I turned my head just in time to see a flash of black dart between the trees. My breath caught.

He was moving, prowling, hunting me like prey.

I felt a rush of adrenaline push me forward. I had to get away. I took a deep breath, summoning all of what little courage I had, and bolted from my hiding spot, sprinting deeper into the woods. The ground felt uneven beneath my feet, roots threatening to trip me, but I didn't care. I just needed to put distance between us, get back to my car.

Run. Run. RUN, STACEY.

Branches whipped against my arms and face, but I ignored the sting. My lungs burned, but I pressed on, desperate to find safety from this twisted nightmare I suddenly found myself in.

"Here, kitty, kitty," His voice boomed through the trees, playful yet dark, and I glanced back, catching a glimpse of him. The mask glinted in the moonlight, his eyes shining like a predator's.

My stomach turned and I took a deep gulp of air so I didn't throw up. I had to focus. I could outsmart him. I could—

A sudden rustle behind me broke my concentration, and I stumbled, losing my footing. I fell hard, the ground jarring my knees and tearing my fishnets as I hit the earth. My breath left me in a rush, and I turned to see him behind me.

The mask loomed closer, and panic surged through me.

His voice was dripping with excitement as he reached for me.

"Gotcha."

Chapter 5
Zach

I lunged forward, grasping her arm as she tried to scramble away from me. The thrill of the chase, the scent of her fear mixed with something else, something intoxicating, flooded my senses and my cock threatened to spill right there.

I pulled her in close, feeling her heart race against my chest.

"You're not Matt," she gasped, her eyes frantic as she tried to push against me.

I grinned behind the mask, reveling in her confusion and the delicious spike of adrenaline that pulsed through me. "No, I'm not."

She struggled against my grip, but I held her tighter, the warmth of her skin seeping into mine through our clothes. The pheromones of a witch, I realized, were unlike anything I'd ever experienced. They sank deep into my lungs making my head spin with an insane need to devour every inch of her.

"Let me go," she demanded, but her voice wavered, betraying the fear that lingered beneath her bravado.

I leaned in closer, inhaling deeply, letting her scent wash over me. She made me feel like I was high on the most illicit drugs. I wanted to drown in it, to lose myself in her. I'd happily overdose on that pussy and have her begging for death right along with me.

"I can't do that," I murmured, my breath brushing against her ear through my mask. "Not when I've finally caught you."

"What do you want?"

I didn't answer, not with words. Instead, I let my actions speak for me. I trailed my fingers along her jaw, marveling at the softness of her skin. She trembled beneath my touch, and I could feel the rapid beat of her pulse, the way her breath hitched in her throat.

"You," I breathed.

She stilled, her eyes searching mine through the mask. I knew she couldn't see me, not really, but in that moment, I felt exposed, stripped bare by the intensity of her gaze.

"Who are you?"

I hesitated.

"Just someone who likes to have a little fun."

Stacey glared at me. "Well, this isn't fun."I chuckled. "I beg to differ."

The anger that shone in her honey brown eyes was adorable but I took mercy on her.

The real game was about to begin, after all.

"Zach," I said softly. "My name is Zach."

"Zach?" She spat the name like it left a bad taste in her mouth. "You mean the guy I just had drinks with? *That* fucking guy?"

The mask I wore felt heavy, but not as heavy as the weight of her gaze. The power radiating off her body hummed in the air, and I groaned, the sound escaping me before I could swallow it down. She took that as a sign I was distracted, and she was right. She punched me right in the chest and I coughed out a laugh.

"What's wrong?" she shot back, a hint of a smirk curling her lips. "Too much for you to handle?"

I fought the urge to push her to the ground and drive myself into her, driven by a need I didn't fully understand. Her violence didn't deter me. No, instead, it ignited something primal from within.

"You don't know what you're dealing with," I said, forcing the words out.

Her laughter danced through the air, sharp and taunting. "And you do? What, you think you can just chase strangers through the woods and get away with it?"

I tightened my grip on her arm, feeling the sinewy muscle beneath my fingers. The connection between us sparked, electric and undeniable. I could almost see a light radiating off her skin. Interesting.

"I do when they're meant to be mine."

She arched an eyebrow, defiance blazing in her eyes. "Yours? Is this some sick joke you play on women during Halloween? Am I some sort of trophy?"

"Not a trophy," I replied, my voice low. "More like the key to a puzzle I can't seem to solve when you look at me like that."

She bit her bottom lip, and for a brief moment, the tension between us shifted. I caught the flicker of something in her expression—was it curiosity? Want? The way her body trembled told me she felt it too, the tension coiling tighter, threatening to snap like all the twigs we'd ruined on our chase.

"Then figure me out," she challenged, her tone daring, but I knew she was still terrified. I could smell it almost more than her arousal.

"Trust me," I said, my voice dropping to a whisper, "I intend to."

I leaned in, but before I could close the distance, a sharp pain exploded in my gut. Stacey's knee connected with brutal force, knocking the wind out of me. I stumbled back, gasping for air.

She didn't waste a second. With a burst of speed, she tore away from me, darting back into the dense woods around us. Her footsteps faded quickly, leaving me alone with the ache in my abdomen and the lingering scent of her magic.

"Damn it," I growled, frustration bubbling up inside me.

I glanced down at my watch, the glowing numbers mocking me. 8:04 PM. Time was slipping away faster than I'd anticipated and this game of cat and mouse was dragging on too long.

I'd thought it would be simple. Catch her, complete the mating ritual, handle the sacrifice, and still have time for a little fun before midnight struck. But Stacey was proving to be more than just a pretty face with a magical aura. She was cunning, quick, and far too elusive for my liking.

Fuck, how I wanted her.

Sighing, I pushed myself up, ignoring the twinge of pain from where she'd struck me. I had to admire her spirit, even if it was complicating my plans. Luckily for me, I still had a good amount of my own demonic qualities even though I inhabited this human body. The fast healing being a top favorite, for sure.

"Here, kitty kitty," I called out, my voice echoing through the trees. "Come out, come out, wherever you are."

I moved deeper into the woods, my eyes scanning the shadows for any sign of movement. The forest was alive with nighttime sounds – rustling leaves, chirping crickets, the distant hoot of an owl. But no Stacey.

"You can't hide forever, little witch," I said, a hint of amusement in my voice. "We both know how this ends."

The ache in my gut was gone now and I moved deeper into the forest. The night air was thick with the scent of pine and dirt, but underneath it all, I could still catch traces of Stacey's delicious aroma. It pulled at me, urging me forward like a siren's call and bringing me in the right direction.

I paused, listening for any sign of her, but nothing betrayed her location. Frustration gnawed at me. Time was ticking.

"I'm going to get that pussy if it's the last thing I do in this fucking body."

Every rustle of leaves, every snapping twig made me whip my head around, hoping to catch a glimpse of her. But the forest seemed to be conspiring against me, hiding her from view. As I pushed through a dense thicket, a flash of movement caught my eye. I froze, my heart racing. There, just ahead, I saw a flicker of pale skin disappearing behind a large oak tree.

"Mine," I whispered.

I crept forward, careful to avoid any loose twigs or dry leaves that might give me away. I was close now, so close I could almost taste victory.

As I rounded the tree, ready to grab her, I found... nothing. The spot where I'd seen her was empty, save for a few fallen leaves stirred by the wind.

"Damn it," I hissed, spinning around.

That's when I heard it - a soft giggle, barely audible over the ambient forest noise. It came from somewhere to my left, deeper in the woods.

"Oh, you think this is funny?" I called out, unable to keep the mixture of frustration and admiration from my voice. "Just wait until I catch you, little witch. We'll see who's laughing then."

I was starting to enjoy the challenge more than I cared to admit.

The sound of her laughter, like a silver bell, rang through the forest, drawing me closer. My heart raced as I stalked her, relishing the chase, the game that only we knew we were playing.

"Zach," she called out, her voice playful, taunting. "Is that all you've got?"

I stopped in my tracks, the sound of my name on her lips disorienting. "I have more than you can probably take."

Silence. The forest held its breath with her.

"Stacey," I whispered. "Time to come out."

First, I heard a sigh and then I saw her. Standing amidst the trees, her eyes sparkling with defiance, her chest heaving from the exertion of our game. She was beautiful, wild, and seemingly unafraid.

Our eyes locked, a silent challenge passing between us.

"Let's end this, shall we?" I said, taking another step forward.

She turned, ready to run again, but I was faster. I lunged, grabbing her arm, and spun her toward me. She struggled, but I held her tight, my body pressed against hers, the swell of her breasts pressing into my chest.

"Please," she begged, her voice shaking.

I smiled, the mask hiding my expression, but my eyes burned with the thoughts of what I planned to do with her. "I was hoping you'd beg."

I pushed her against a nearby tree, the impact knocking the breath from her lungs. I tilted the mask up to rest on my head, exposing my face and she gasped. Not wanting to waste such an opportunity, I took full advantage, covering her mouth with mine. The kiss was fierce, savage, a clash of tongues and teeth. Her hands scrambled against my chest, trying to push me away, but I held her firm, my lips claiming hers with a desperation that I never had for another woman in over 200 years.

Her struggles weakened, and I felt her body press against me, the resistance melting away. My hands roamed, exploring the curves of her body, pulling at her torn sweater and gripping at her hips. Her breath came in ragged pants, and I knew she was close to breaking. Close to giving in.

I pulled away, and I knew from her expression that she caught the way my eyes glowed when my demon form threatened to break free.

"Zach," she breathed, and I shuddered at the sound of my name on her lips. "What are you?"

I leaned in, my lips brushing her ear. "Your worst nightmare."

Chapter 6
Stacey

8:25 P.M.
Halloween

I wanted to back away, to put space between us, but something held me there, a weird feeling that I couldn't explain. "What do you mean?"

His eyes burned into mine, and he reached out, his fingers brushing my cheek. "You're different, like me. You feel it, don't you?"

I nodded even though I didn't know what 'different' actually meant.

"Let me show you," he whispered, his lips inches from mine. "Let me show you what we can do together."

His fingers tangled in my hair, pulling me closer, and I couldn't resist him any longer. My hands found his shoulders, and I returned the kiss with everything in me. I felt his smile against my lips, a hint of triumph, and it only fueled how badly I wanted this man before me.

Zach's mouth trailed down my neck and I arched against him, my breath coming in sharp gasps as his lips and tongue left a trail of pure heat on my skin. His hands slid down my body, cupping my thighs, lifting my core against the bulge in his pants as he pressed me into the tree.

I tried to break away, my head falling back as I gasped for air. "Wait—*no*—" But my words were cut off by his mouth on mine again, fierce and demanding.

Then suddenly, he tore away the fishnet stockings at my crotch, his fingers skillful and quick. I heard a sharp intake of breath as he realized I wasn't wearing anything underneath. His eyes met mine, dark and hungry but still glowing this unnatural green, and he smirked.

"*Bad kitty.*"

Before I could respond, he dropped to his knees before me, his eyes never leaving mine.

His long fingers curled around my knees, drawing me closer, and my heart hammered in my chest. I could feel his breath on my skin, and tried to push on his shoulders.

"Don't be afraid," he murmured, his voice low and husky. "I just like to play with my food before I eat it."

I stared down at him as my cunt throbbed with a need I had never felt before. Not once, with all the guys I had been with. I wanted to trust the intensity in his eyes, but I held back, unsure of what to expect from him next. His thumbs stroked my skin, sending goosebumps up my legs as he slowly slid my skirt higher.

God, that felt good.

I bit my lip, trying to suppress a moan.

Then his fingers found my wet slit, and he parted me as he watched my reaction. I knew I was way too wet for a woman who should be fearing for her life, and he was figuring that out now as he soaked his fingers with my slick.

His thumb swirled a few lazy circles around my clit and I felt exposed, vulnerable, and yet, I didn't want him to stop.

Zach's mouth found my inner thigh as he lifted a leg over his shoulder, and he kissed the sensitive skin, his teeth nipping at the skin there. "So beautiful," he murmured, his lips moving higher. "So perfect."

My hands found his shoulders, my fingers clutching at him as if he wasn't some stranger who had impersonated my boyfriend and hunted me through the woods.

"Do you know why you haven't been able to cum, little kitty?" he asked as he continued to trail his rough fingertips through my folds.

My brows furrowed and I pushed at his shoulders as I tried to get him to look up at me. "How do you know that?"

The grin that stretched across his full lips was a slow one.

"I know a lot more than that," he said, and pinched my clit hard. I moaned out a curse as he rolled my clit gently between two fingers. "Like how you keep holding back those powers of yours. Sex is tied to power and you've had it in spades all this time."

And then his mouth was where I secretly craved it, and I arched against him, a strangled cry escaping my throat. He devoured me with a tongue so hungry that it was like being worshiped and tortured at the same time. My legs trembled but he held me up against the tree as he lavished my pussy with the most ravenous affection.

I couldn't think, couldn't breathe—I existed only in that moment, lost in the feeling of how his mouth closed around the sensitive bundle of nerves only to suck it into his mouth and roll his tongue over it. Every touch, every kiss, every flick of his tongue pushed me closer to the edge. I was teetering on the edge of what could only be an orgasm and I whispered his name like a prayer.

"That's it," he whispered against my heated flesh. "Let it go, witch. Let yourself feel that energy builds inside you and release it."

"I- I don't know how," I sobbed as I bucked my hips against his face, desperate for more of his mouth on me. I felt like I was about to leave my body and I was terrified. Even more scared than when I was running from him in the woods.

His response was to thrust two fingers into me, claiming me, owning me, and I yelped as they hit a spot I hadn't known existed. "Just focus. Imagine your body being full of a million tiny butterflies that want to break free. Let them out of that little cage and," he paused as he sucked on my clit in tandem with his thrusting fingers before continuing, "Set. Them. Free."

I did as he commanded—not in the position to do anything but listen to this man that was literally about to do what no man or even myself had been able to. Gasping, I envisioned the release he asked of me, and it was like something inside me snapped. I felt it in the blood that screamed in my veins, in the pit of my chest, on my skin...

My *skin*...

It was... glowing?

There was a fine mist that seemed to be coming off my body and he grinned up at me from between my legs before winking at me. "That's my girl."

I swayed where I stood and he dove back between my legs on a mission. I cried out as I felt his tongue push against my entrance and then somehow make its way inside me. It was so far inside I swear it was licking that spot he had found with his fingers moments before. I grinded against his face by pulling onto the hood of his sweatshirt for leverage and begged him to stop. I surely wouldn't survive what was coming next.

But he didn't stop. He continued to push further in and pleasure me, drawing out the sensations until I was mindless, boneless, my body his to command.

It was too much, too overwhelming, and I tried to push him away, my hands against his shoulders. "Please—I can't—" His tongue twisted inside me and made my breath catch. I cried out, my body arching into him.

I can't.

I can't

I can't.

And then...

I did. I shattered, crying out his name, my body convulsing with the force of my orgasm. Darkness blurred at the edges of my vision, and I felt myself falling backward against the tree, defeated and weak as I stared down at him. I was sobbing and the purple light around me pulsed like it was alive.

"Yes," Zach whispered, and I swear I saw an elongated forked tongue make its way back inside his mouth as his hot breath fanned the wetness between my thighs. Impossible. My mind must have broken. "Give it all to me, Stacey. Let me drink every drop of power from this pussy."

I continued to cry, so shaken from achieving what I'd come to think was impossible. I started to slide down the tree, the bark tearing deeper into my sweater, but he caught me, holding me against him.

"You did so good, little witch," he murmured, his lips brushing my neck. "So *damn* good."

I sagged against him, and didn't care if I was in the arms of a stranger.

It felt like I'd died already.

"Let's get this finished," he said, his voice gentle.

I didn't want to move, didn't want to break the spell that enveloped us. But I felt dazed, like I'd stepped out of a dream, and I couldn't help but wonder if this was real. All of my energy was gone and the purple haze had dwindled to almost nothing. I wanted to ask what happened, where that had come from. But I had never felt so exhausted in my life.

I barely registered the flicker of movement as he pulled the mask back over his face, the fabric shadowing his features. It felt surreal, the way my body fit in his arms, cozy and trusting.

8:25 P.M. Halloween

Far from the chase that had led us here.

I wanted to fight against the dizziness that threatened to swallow me whole, but my limbs felt like lead.

"Zach," I murmured, but the name slipped through my lips like the colored smoke, lost in the haze.

He lifted me effortlessly, cradling me against him. "Come on, kitten," he whispered, and I was vaguely aware of him carrying me out of the woods.

Suddenly, I found myself in the passenger seat of a sleek, black car. The leather was cool against my skin, and I shivered as reality settled back in, pulling at the frayed edges of what sanity still hung in my mind. I tried to sit up, to protest, but it was like I was drugged.

"Zach, I don't want to die," I managed to say, my voice slurring together like a bad dream. Panic clawed at my throat, and I strained against the seat belt that he'd just fastened that held me in place.

He crouched beside me in the space where the car door was still open, his masked face slipping out of focus. "I'm not here to kill you," he said, his voice steady and calm. "I promise."

I squinted at him as I tried to stay conscious. "Then what do you want?"

"Your soul," he murmured, and those were the last words I heard before everything went black.

Chapter 7
Zach

I looked over at Stacey's sleeping form as I got in the driver's seat and my fingers itched to grab her, to pull her back into the shadows of the trees and taste her again. Bathe in her power, so willing to mix with mine.

But I had eternity to play with Stacey.

I had to take care of business first.

Stacey had no idea of the power she possessed, locked away inside that delectable body. It was a shame, really. I thought she was faking it, but after the texts I read between her friends about not being able to orgasm and the fact she didn't set me on fire the moment she realized she was in danger proved me wrong. She really was unaware, blind to the magic within herself. Had her parents hidden her true nature from her? Kept her from the truth? Didn't they know it led to her breaking down? Up until now it had been sexual in nature, but it could have led to more physical defects.

Well, it didn't matter now. I had gotten through to her. I'd felt her power when I'd lapped at that dripping cunt, and I wanted more. I needed to consume it all.

I'd prepared a place for us, a large and private estate where I could keep her safe and all to myself. It was perfect, secluded and remote. The family who'd lived there previously had been more than willing to sell and disappear when I showed up this morning. They'd taken my money and run, no questions asked. Left that nice car here, too.

Centuries of existence–albeit mostly spent in hell–had taught me that money and power went hand in hand. One could always be exchanged for the other. And I had plenty of both.

I reached out, my fingers brushing her cheek, and she leaned into my touch, her eyes fluttering closed.

"That's it, little witch. You're almost mine."

I put the car in gear and pulled away, my eyes never leaving Stacey's thighs where her cum still lingered between them. The sound of the engine purred like a cat, matching my companion's attire as I watched her shift unconsciously, the movement drawing my eyes back down to the glistening proof of the pleasure my demon tongue had brought her. I licked my lips, tasting her once again in my mind.

The night air whipped through the open car windows, carrying the scent of fall—a mixture of dead leaves and distant bonfires. It was a reminder that time was passing, the world was turning, and soon the hard part would come.

But for now, it was just me and Stacey, alone in the darkness.

As we drove out of the woods and passed through the neighboring towns, I kept a careful eye out for any signs of life. The streets were mostly empty, except for the occasional few on their way home.

I caught sight of a clock tower as I slowed for a stop sign. 10:03p.m.

My gaze flicked back to Stacey, and I felt a surge of possession as I noticed the way she'd moved in her sleep. The position of her thighs as they parted was an invitation I couldn't resist. I reached out, my fingers tracing the soft skin of her leg, trailing upwards. Her breath hitched, and she murmured something unintelligible, her eyes still closed.

The sound of laughter snapped me back to the present, and I realized we'd stopped in front of a group of kids. I stared at them through the mask, the glow of my eyes still engaged from being so ungodly turned on. They didn't notice, too caught up in their candy-fueled excitement.

I pushed my hunger down. We were almost to the house, and I needed to be prepared for anything. After all, I wasn't the only creature of the night out here looking to nab a witch, and I'd be damned if anyone was going to take Stacey from me now.

My beautiful witch, my little scaredy cat.

She had every right to be scared, of course.

Considering I was about to claim her for eternity.

Chapter 8
Stacey

10:33 P.M.
Halloween

I jolted awake and started coughing against the hard-wood floor beneath me. Panic shot through my veins as I struggled to move. My wrists and ankles throbbed with pressure, tight ropes biting into my skin.

"Zach?" I croaked, my voice a dry whisper that barely escaped my lips. I twisted my head, searching for any sign of him, but found only shadows dancing in the corners of the dimly lit room. My heart pounded as I squinted, trying to make sense of where I was.

Something heavy scraped across the floor. The sound echoed in the large room which looked vaguely like my parent's drawing room, only with actual color as I made out the red curtains on the windows. My pulse quickened as I turned my head toward the sound which was really hard considering I was bound and set on my stomach, chest to the floor. The figure dragging whatever it was moved with a purpose that sent a chill down my spine.

"Please," I managed to gasp, though the word felt foreign on my tongue. "What are you doing?"

The man stopped abruptly, his silhouette shifting in and out of focus. He crouched down, revealing just enough detail to send a wave of dread crashing over me. My breath hitched when I recognized him—Zach's red skull mask glinted under the flickering overhead lights.

"What are you—"

Before I could finish, he straightened up again and resumed pulling whatever it was at his feet closer to me. It seemed too big to be just an object; it looked almost as big as Zach.

A low laugh slipped from his lips, rich and dark like chocolate but laced with something sinister.

"It's okay," he said smoothly, but the edge in his tone made my skin crawl. "You'll understand soon enough."

My vision blurred again, spinning as confusion clouded my mind. I wanted to scream or kick against the bindings that held me captive—but all I could manage was a weak tug against them as I pushed my breasts into the floor for leverage.

"Don't hurt yourself," he said, sarcastically. And God, did that make me so mad. He was so unhinged, so unbothered about everything he was doing and my fear was quickly turning to rage.

"Sorry, I forgot you wanted to do the honors," I hissed.

"I'm not trying to hurt you," he sighed and paused in his task to look at me. "Remember how I took you out, fulfilled your depraved fantasy - *that* was quite fun for me, though. And then I made you cum all over my lips and brought you someplace nice?"

"This is 'nice'?"

"Just going to skip over the mind-blowing orgasm part, then?"

I snarled at him and he laughed as I twisted in my binds. When I continued to thrash on the floor, I noticed that purple haze again and so did Zach. He dropped the figure and started walking toward me across the room.

"Now, now. Don't get worked up, I'm not ready for you yet. I still have to finish setting up."

"Get me out of these freakin' ropes!"

"I can't do that yet, silly kitty."

This fucker. He was almost to me when I cried out, "I want these ropes off now!"

All of a sudden I felt the tension around my limbs loosen and I was freed.

Even though the mask hid his expression, I could see him hesitate as he approached me.

Shocked by how I had undone the binds, I slowly pushed myself onto my knees and we stared at each other as I gathered the courage to bolt. Zach put his hands up as if he was ready to tame a wild animal.

"Stacey," Zach murmured, only a couple feet from me. "You don't know what you're capable of right now, sweetheart. I'm going to need you to calm down."

My hands flexed against the ground as I tilted my head at him. "Or what?"

"Or, I'll have to force you."

I glared at him and my eyes darted to the door I could see in the distance past Zach. I pushed myself to my feet in one quick motion and made to dash past him but he caught me easily even as I fought him. I felt the headband that held my cat ears slip down as I struggled.

"Let go!" I yelled, but he held me up in front of him with his large hands wrapped around my biceps.

"Stacey, I'm sorry."

I paused in my fight to look up at him, the pain in his voice catching me off-guard.

"For what?" I asked.

I heard the sigh behind his mask, but it was his unnatural glowing green eyes that had me listening intently to what he'd say next.

"For this."

Zach's head came down to connect with mine and I barely registered the pain of the impact before I was knocked out.

Chapter 9
Zach

10:40 P.M.
Halloween

*S*hit.

Chapter 10
Stacey

I woke to Zach's voice, a dark, low rumble in the dimly-lit room.

"Wakie wakie, little kitty."

The sound of his voice sent a shudder through me, and my eyes snapped open. I let out a startled scream as I was met with the terrifying red skull mask just inches from my face. His unnatural green eyes glared down at me, and I tried to scramble back, but my head pounded so I just sat there clutching it in pain.

Zach threw his head back and laughed, the sound echoing around the vast room. His eyes, framed by the mask's jagged eyeholes, glinted with amusement.

"Scared you, didn't I, sweetheart? And this is just a mask. My real form is so much worse. I'd love to see the look on your face if you ever saw it."

I swallowed hard, my throat dry.

"What are you then?" I asked.

"A demon," he whispered seductively. "But I wasn't always."

I heard him move around the room to a place behind me but couldn't open my eyes yet against the screaming pain in my head.

I was so close to getting out... And he... That bastard fucking headbutted me. Who *does* that?

"A long time ago," he spoke softly, and the sounds of a piano began to play. "I was an ordinary man. Extremely good-looking, of course. But I loved music. God, how I loved it. My mother was the one who taught me growing up and when it came time to help my father who made clothing for a living, I refused. I was so sure that I could make it on my talents, but we didn't have social media back in the 1700s, so it was hard to get the word out."

The music stopped momentarily like he was waiting for me to laugh at his joke.

I didn't.

"I was also competing against Mozart, and Beethoven - Bach had at least passed on by then." But they were alive over 200 years ago, that can't be right. I heard him sigh as he started playing again, but it wasn't anything I recognized.

"Long lifetime short, I was approached by a man in black one night. Offered me everything I could want but I would be of service once I died to the keeper of hell. I had one incredible night in London and overnight I was a sensation. And then, on my way to France to play for Louis XVI, I fell ill and died. Exactly 2 weeks from the time I sold my soul. And I've been trying to get my life back ever since."

I found myself turning to look at him as he continued to move his strong fingers along the ivory keys. He would have looked sexy, sitting at the black grand piano in nothing but a pair of black dress pants. If it weren't for the damn mask he was still wearing.

Oh, who was I kidding. It was *still* sexy.

He looked up at me and tilted his head. "I'm sorry, this is probably quite dated for you."

Turning his attention back to the piano, he began playing a different tune and my jaw hung open in surprise. Zach chuckled as he stole a glance at me and continued playing.

"Is that... Are you playing Taylor Swift right now?"

Zach didn't answer me but instead just kept banging out the chorus to *Look What You Made Me Do*. After a few more seconds, he stopped and looked at me again. "The *Reputation* album is my favorite. Which one is yours?"

I sputtered, "What?"

"A true musician recognizes another. Now, which is your favorite album?"

I brushed some of my hair out of my face to look at him better before finally whispering, "Evermore."

I jumped as Zach clapped his hands enthusiastically and laughed. "I should have known. Pictured you more as a *Midnights* girl this morning, but this makes sense, too."

"I haven't listened to her in a while," I tell him and I don't know why I'm telling him this. "My boyfriends all hated her so I was forbidden to play her music around them."

Zach pointed to the area in front of where I was seated on the floor and said, "Like that asshole?"

That's when I noticed Matt. He was lying on the ground nearby, tied up like I was earlier, unmoving.

"Is he... is he dead?" I croaked out, fearing the answer.

Zach shook his head, his mask rustling slightly with the movement. "Not yet. That's up to you, little kitty. You get to decide his fate."

My heart sank, and the weight of his words crushed me. "What do you mean? I don't understand."

Zach chuckled, a deep, menacing sound that sent a chill running through me.

"Oh, you'll understand soon enough. For now, I just know that his life is in your hands. Literally."

I felt sick, my stomach twisting with fear and dread. Immediately I felt the need to bolt again but I couldn't carry a grown man out of here. "Please... just let us go. We won't tell anyone about this. We won't—"

"Shhh," Zach cut in, raising a finger to his masked lips and he got up from the piano to walk towards me. "We both know that's not true. Now, enough talk. It's time for your first test, little kitty. Are you ready to play?"

I wanted to beg, to plead, but the glint in his eye told me it would be useless. My mind raced as I tried to process what was happening, but one thought kept repeating:

What kind of game were we playing, and how could I save us both?

I stared at Zach, my heart hammering in my chest. The mask hid his expressions, but his voice, deep and gravelly, reminded me how much I was actually in danger.

"Ready?"

"For the first test?" I asked, my voice shaking despite my efforts to stay calm. "What do you want from me?"

Zach took a menacing step forward, and I flinched, unable to suppress a small whimper.

"Oh, kitty, you'll soon find out. But first, let's set you straight. I want you to play fairly."

With a quick motion, he knelt before me and placed his hands on my head, making sure to straighten my cat ears as he did so. Almost at once, the pounding in my head vanished. When he pulled away, I rubbed at my temples where it had a tingling feeling, all while keeping my eyes on Zach.

"I don't have full use of my powers in this form, but I do have some." He shrugged, like that explained everything.

I watched him as he retrieved a ceremonial knife from a nearby marble table. The blade glinted in the dim light as he twirled it in his hand, then held it out, offering it to me, hilt first. The knife was an ornate, bronze blade, its surface engraved with intricate patterns.

"Take it, little kitty. This is your first test. You must draw blood."

I hesitated, my eyes flicking to Matt's still form.

"Go on," Zach coaxed. "Take the knife. You have five minutes to make your choice. Whose blood will it be? Yours or his?"

I shook my head, my eyes stinging with unshed tears. "I won't hurt him or myself. Just let us go."

Zach's eyes, and unblinking, held mine.

"Time is ticking."

I wanted to scream, to rage at him, but something in his gaze held me captive. I felt the weight of his words, and my mind raced as I tried to process the impossible decision he was forcing upon me.

The seconds ticked by like hours, and my heart pounded in my ears.

My eyes darted to Matt. I could see his chest rising and falling in a slow, even rhythm. He was still alive, for now.

"Please," I whispered, my voice hoarse. "Just tell me what you want."

Zach's lips curled upwards, his mask hiding the full extent of his smile, but I could hear it when he spoke next.

"It's simple. I want to see if you have what it takes."

"Fuck you!" The words burst from my lips, fueled by anger and desperation.

Zach's laughter filled the room once more, the sound grating against my nerves. The skull mask tilted backward as he roared with amusement, and for a moment, I imagined ripping that mask from his face and punching him in his pretty face.

"My, my, such language. Aren't we feisty? Kitty's got claws, it seems. That's exactly what I wanted to hear."

I frowned, confusion clouding my brown eyes. "What do you mean?"

"It's all part of the game, sweetheart. You showed me that you have spirit, that you're not willing to just roll over and accept your fate. That's admirable, really."

I growled at him. "Then that should suffice. Let's move on."

Zach's eyes narrowed, and his voice turned cold and cruel. "All in good time, witch. For now, just know that you're here to play. And the rules are simple: you must draw blood."

"Never. I won't play your sick game," I spat, my eyes flicking to Matt's unmoving form. "Just let him go. He has nothing to do with this."

"Ah, but he does," Zach replied, his voice silky smooth. "You see, this game is all about choices and consequences. Will you let him live and damn yourself or kill him and keep your power?"

"Why do you keep talking about my 'power'?" My voice quavered, but I stood my ground, facing the man, the *thing* before me.

Zach's mask tilted to the side, as if he were considering me with newfound interest. "I'm disappointed, little kitty. Your parents never told you the truth?"

I shook my head, my mind racing. What was he talking about?

"You mean there's never been weird things that have happened when you've been upset or excited?" He took a step toward me, his looming figure filling my vision. "Strange occurrences that you couldn't explain?"

I swallowed hard, my eyes darting around the room as I tried to keep my composure. My gaze focused back on the piano to ground myself. I recalled a few moments—the time the lights had flickered and died when I'd argued with my parents, or the way the wind had kicked up, shaking the windows as if in anger, when I'd been thrilled at a concert. But I couldn't bring myself to acknowledge them. "I don't know what you mean."

Zach's eyes narrowed, and for a moment, I thought I saw a flash of anger in their dark depths. "Don't lie to me, pussycat. You've felt different for a long time. It's a shame your parents never taught you how to wield it."

Finally, I found my voice, laced with a hint of anger. "They're not my real parents. I was adopted." The words tumbled out, and I bit my lip, immediately wishing I could take them back.

Zach stilled, his mask hiding any emotion, but his body language shifted, becoming less confrontational. "Adopted, you say? That explains their neglect. They should have prepared you for your true destiny. Maybe you wouldn't be bound up before a demon right now if they had."

"What destiny?" I asked, my voice laced with a mixture of fear and annoyance. "My parents never mentioned anything about powers or special abilities. Is that why you keep calling me a witch?" I burst out laughing, the sound echoing absurdly in the vast room. "That's crazy."

Zach didn't laugh with me. Instead, he stepped closer, reaching out as if to touch me, but then let his hand drop to his side. "God, you have so much to learn. And we have so little time."

My heart sank, and the weight of his words hit me like a physical blow. "What do you mean?"

Zach's eyes glinted, and his voice turned low and menacing. "All you need to do is be willing to give me what I want."

"By tying us up and threatening us? How is that going to make me willing to help you?"

Zach stepped back, as if considering me from a new perspective. "True, true. I may have been a little hasty. I also did give you the first orgasm of your life so there's that." I cursed at him and he folded his arms across his naked chest. "Perhaps a deal, then. I offer you knowledge—an understanding of your power, I can even let you keep it if we get rid of old Matt here—and in return, you give me your word that you'll consider my proposal."

I hesitated, unsure if I could trust this strange, menacing figure. But the offer of knowledge was tempting, and the desire to understand the strange occurrences that had haunted me for years was too great. My need for power was growing from feeling so helpless and taking over any semblance of sanity.

"Very well," Zach said, taking my silence as agreement. "The deal is struck. Now, let's get started, shall we?"

Leaving my question unanswered was infuriating. "Started with what?"

My mind whirled as I recalled the events leading up to our abduction. Let's get chased in the fucking forest. Let's allow a stranger to tongue fuck you against a tree. I mean, my friends were absolutely right—How had I been so *careless?* Note to self, if I get out of this: Go back to being a boring bitch.

"Come on, Zach, just let him go. He hasn't done any-thing."

"He hasn't, has he?" Zach's tone turned mocking. "He let you and your dark, twisted desires fester because he couldn't step up. Is that why you came so hard on my face in the woods?"

"I won't choose," I stated, my voice steady despite the turmoil within me. "I won't play."

Zach simply lifted the mask briefly to show me his face. And why did his expression scare me more than that mask had? "Your five minutes are up. His blood or your magic?"

I stared at him, my mouth dry, my heart pounding. My gaze dropped to the knife he held out, its bronze surface shimmering.

Blood.

"Fine, I'll play your damn game." I stood and took a menacing step forward, ignoring the tremble in my legs, and snatched the knife from his hand. "I choose him. Let's get this over with."

Zach's eyes glittered with a mix of triumph and dark amusement before he put the mask back over his face. He moved to stand beside me, his tall form towering over Matt's limp body.

"Atta girl. Now, put it right through his chest. Or slit his throat. Whichever you'd prefer."

My hands shook as I gripped the knife. I took a deep breath, steeling myself, and turned toward Matt. My eyes flickered to his peaceful face, his chest rising and falling gently.

In a swift motion, I pretended to kneel beside him, but instead, I spun on my heels, raising the knife high, aiming for Zach's throat. I put all my weight behind the blow, a scream of frustration and anger tearing from me as I lunged.

Zach was faster. He caught my wrist mid-swing, his grip like iron. The knife clattered to the floor, and I cried out as I watched it drop. He wrenched my arm, twisting it behind my back, forcing a pained gasp from my lips.

"Naughty kitty. Didn't I tell you to choose *wisely?*"

His other arm snaked around my waist, pulling me tight against his chest. I struggled, kicking and squirming, but it was no use. He was too strong.

"Let me go!" I screamed.

Zach chuckled, his breath hot against my ear. "Oh, I will, little kitty. But I need your soul first. We need to speed things up. We're running out of time."

He forced me down, my back crushing against his chest as he pushed me to the ground. My breath left me in a rush as the air was forced from my lungs. I struggled to breathe, panic rising in my chest.

Then I felt his hand on my thigh, hiking up my skirt. Humiliation and rage warred in me as I twisted and bucked backward, trying to free myself from his grip.

"Zach, stop!" I screamed, my voice breaking. "Please, let me go! Don't do this. Don't, *please.*"

But my pleas fell on deaf ears. I heard the sound of a zipper and rustle of his pants and then his hand moved higher, his touch rough and intrusive.

I only felt his fingers at my bare cunt for a moment, spreading my wetness along my opening. When I felt the head of his cock rubbing along my slit, I choked on a gasp because there was definitely something different about it. Was that ... *metal?* Was he pierced? Then he was inside me, filling me, and I cried out because he was definitely pierced at the tip and all the way down in what I could only imagine was the infamous Jacob's Ladder I had read about in romance books. I felt exposed and helpless, my body positioned on all fours over Matt, my fishnets torn and tattered, my judgment shattered.

As Zach thrust into me, a searing pain shot through my body. It was more than just the physical intrusion—it was as if something was tearing inside me, deep within my very soul and it had nothing to do with the piercings and everything to do with the man attached to them.

And then I saw it. A purple aura radiated from my skin, spreading across the room. It was beautiful and terrifying at the same time. It was happening again.

"What... what's happening?" I managed to gasp between his relentless thrusts.

Zach's breathing quickened, becoming more ragged as he drove into me with increasing force."That's your magic, baby. That's you letting it go."

I didn't understand what he was saying. All I knew was the pain and the strange, glowing aura that seemed to be pouring out of me. It was like my body was a vessel, channeling some unknown energy, and I had no control over it.

The purple light grew brighter, filling the room with an otherworldly glow. I felt a surge of power coursing through me, and for a moment, I thought I could break free of Zach's hold. But then his hands gripped my hips tighter, holding me in place as he continued his assault on my pussy.

My cries turned to whimpers as the pleasure and pain blended into an intense, overwhelming sensation. I couldn't believe it, my body betrayed me as it reacted to Zach's touch, even as my mind rebelled against what was happening.

Zach must have felt it too because his grip on me tightened, and his breath quickened against my neck. He tossed the skull mask aside, revealing his face—and I twisted mine just enough to look back at him. Then his teeth sank into the flesh of my neck, and a jolt of pleasure shot through me. His hands found their way under my sweater, expertly finding my nipples through the thin lace of my bra, and he pinched and twisted, sending shocks of sensation straight to my core.

I thrashed and moaned, unable to control the sounds that tore from my throat. It was a heady mix of pain and pleasure, and I felt myself falling deeper under Zach's spell... which was funny to me, seeing as how I was the one who was supposed to be a witch.

But then, beneath me, I felt movement. Matt was stirring, his body twitching as he began to wake from his drugged slumber.

Mortification hit me like a physical blow. I sobbed, my body shaking with the force of my tears. Here I was, helplessly pinned down, being taken by this monster, and the person I had dated all month, was waking up to witness it all.

"No, please, Zach," I begged. "He's waking up. Stop."

But Zach ignored my pleas, his pace only quickening. "Let him watch, little kitty. Let him see what a real man can do with a pussy this fucking *exquisite.*"

I couldn't bear to look at Matt, to see the horror and confusion on his face as he witnessed my defilement. So, I closed my eyes, wishing I could block out the whole world. But the sensations only intensified, and I felt myself spiraling deeper into a vortex of pleasure as Zach's pierced cock stretched me with every thick, hot inch of him.

Zach's breath was ragged against my ear, his growls of pleasure spurring me on. The sounds of our bodies slapping together filled the room, echoing off the walls. I should have been so ashamed. I should have been absolutely appalled by what I was doing. But, I had never felt pleasure like this before... and unlike the demon taking me from behind, I was only human.

My cries turned to mewls of pleasure, and I knew, in that moment, that I was lost. Whatever Zach wanted from me, I would give it. My willpower was gone, replaced by a desperate need for more.

I was panting, my body trembling, and my mind reeling. I felt exposed, used, and yet, I wanted more. The purple aura still flickered around me, and I felt its power coursing through my veins.

Matt stirred again beneath me, and I finally found the strength to look at him. His eyes were open, and they widened in shock and horror as he took in the scene.

"No, Matt, I—" I started, but Zach cut me off.

"Shhh, little kitty. Let him see what he's missed out on by being a tragic piece of shit, shall we?"

Zach's movements slowed for a few moments and I heard something clank behind me as it hit the floor before he was pulling something around my throat. My mouth opened to scream but my head snapped backward from the force of him pulling on the cold leather until we locked eyes.

"I don't have a leash for my pet, so my belt will have to do."

I could do nothing but take in how the belt tightened when he pulled, his eyes unyielding as it drank in my filthy position. The way they flashed like uranium glass under a blacklight should have been terrifying, but I was starting to crave those eyes on mine.

I didn't care that Matt was watching, his eyes wide with shock and disgust. All I could focus on was the overwhelming sensation of Zach inside me, the friction that had me teetering on the edge.

Matt found his voice, his words laced with hatred. *"You sick bitch!* I always knew you were off, but this? What the fuck is wrong with you? You're a freak."

His words sliced through me, but the physical pleasure drowned out the emotional pain. I was hyper aware of Zach's body behind me, the hard muscle of his thighs as they made contact with mine, and the hard thrust of his hips.

Zach lessened the hold on his makeshift leash and allowed some more oxygen back into my lungs but I continued to look back at him. He whispered in my ear, "You can have this forever, little kitty. I can give this to you every night for the rest of your life."

Then I felt it—a knife pressed into my hand. My fingers curled around the hilt, and it was like I had no qualms about doing the unthinkable. The power I felt in that moment was indescribable. I knew I could end it all with a single stroke, and the thought excited me.

Matt's voice, filled with loathing, spurred me on. "Did you hear me? You're a *freak*, Stacey! Always have been. Get the fuck off me, you crazy psychos."

His words cut deep, but instead of hurting me, they fueled the fire burning within. I wanted to show him just how powerful I was, to make him take back every cruel word he'd ever said to me.

Zach sensed my growing need, and he rocked inside me with a delicious rhythm to match how my ass pushed back against him. "That's it. Let it all out. You're so amazing, baby. Such a perfect, sexy witch. Gonna teach you everything."

My breath quickened, and I felt my orgasm building. It was like a dam breaking, a rush of pleasure and power that threatened to overwhelm me. When Zach reached under me to pull one of my breasts from the confines of my bra and sweater so he could grip it tightly as a means to anchor the snaps of his hips, my mind went blank. And in that moment, I knew exactly what I wanted to do.

"Feel my cock, Stacey. Let it heal this part of you. Embrace what was always meant to be yours. Let me fuck the past right out of this perfect pussy."

That was it. The magic words.

As my climax crashed over me, I lunged forward, knife in hand, and drove it straight into Matt's chest. I felt the blade sink in, and the feel of Matt's heartbeat through his chest mimicked the pulse of my pussy throbbing with release. The room seemed to spin as my orgasm took over, and I cried out, unable to contain magical energy that made the room light up in a hazy lavender explosion of light.

Zach held me tight as I rode out my orgasm, his hands gentle on my body. It was such a stark contrast to the brutality of what I'd just done that my vision blurred. The knife protruded from Matt's chest, and I watched, mesmerized, as blood began to bloom on his shirt.

Matt's eyes went wide, and his mouth opened and closed as if he couldn't quite process what had happened. I watched as blood pooled in his mouth and he choked on the crimson liquid as it flooded his lungs. I always thought he'd OD, but here I was - drunk on my own kind of drug, killing him instead. Then, the gurgling that held my attention stopped and his eyes glazed over.

"You did it," Zach breathed, his voice hoarse.

"You chose."

Chapter 11
Zach

I knew the moment she came that Matt was a goner. The way her sweet cunt clenched around me like a velvet vice was enough to spell it out for me. Stacey was almost mine, and she'd proven it with that knife. The girl had power, and with me, she'd have more than she ever dreamed of.

I thrust harder, my hands gripping her hips, and pulled her down onto Matt's lifeless body. Her scream of release turned to a sob as I pushed her face into the wound she'd created, marking her with his blood.

It was a consecration of sorts—a bloody baptism into a new life. With me.

Her sobs vibrated through her body, and I felt her walls tighten even more around me. The pressure combined with the flesh of her pussy tugging at the piercings on my cock was too much for any part of my psyche to withstand. I pounded into her one last time, feeling myself explode within her. I gripped her hips hard enough to leave bruises, my own body trembling with the force of my climax.

Then, spent, I slipped out of her, our fluids mingling and dripping down her thighs. I turned her onto her back, and finally, I got a good look at her face. Her eyes were wild, a mixture of exhaustion and horror, as she stared at Matt's body.

There was a new energy about her, an aura that practically radiated off her porcelain skin. The purple mist swirled and writhed around her in full force, a tangible manifestation of the power she now possessed.

Stacey's breath came in ragged gasps, and her eyes flickered to me, then down to where I'd just withdrawn from her body. I saw the moment she realized what we'd done, and a shudder ran through her.

"It's okay, little kitty," I whispered, and spoke to her tenderly to soothe her. "He deserved it. You are meant for so much more. Like me. And now, you and I - we're bound together."

The look on her face—it was priceless. I couldn't hold back my satisfied smile as she realized the weight of her actions.

Fuck, humanity was so wretched and I *loved it.*

She was mine, body and soon her fucking soul.

And the best part? She'd done it all of her own free will.

Her eyes flicked back to Matt, and she seemed to realize something. "His soul..." She reached out a shaking hand to touch the dead man's chest where the knife was still embedded, as if she could feel the soul lingering within.

I smirked. "Souls don't just disappear, Stacey. They're powerful things, and now you've got one as a bargaining chip."

Stacey's expression was a mix of awe and fear as she considered the implications of what I'd just told her. "What do I do with it?" she whispered.

Reaching out, I ran a finger down her blood-streaked cheek. "That, my little kitty, is to appease the devil. You'll present this to him as a token of your loyalty, and I won't have to completely drain you of your abilities."

I could see the reluctance in her eyes, the fear of fully committing to the path she'd started down. Stacey was a smart one, probably thinking about the consequences of her actions.

"You're special, Stacey. I wouldn't pick just anyone to spend my existence with. But you..." I gestured to the chaotic scene we'd created, "You're something else. I can make you stronger than you ever thought possible. We have a connection now, one that is deeper than anything you can imagine."

She pulled at her torn sweater and tried to push her skirt down to hide the fluids that clung to her thighs there. Her eyes darted to Matt's body, and she shivered. "Do I have to... will there be more... like him?"

My lips twisted into a smirk and I leaned forward to straighten the cat ears on top of her head. "Killing is my forte, not yours, little kitty. You won't have to get your hands dirty again unless, of course, you want to. It can even be fun, a rush of power that you won't find anywhere else."

I reached down and tilted her chin up, my thumb brushing her lower lip. "Give yourself to me, Stacey. Bind your soul to mine."

Her eyes, wide and terrified, searched my face. Under normal circumstances, we could have talked about this. But, Halloween was almost over.

"I'm not boring you, am I?" I glanced at my watch—11:49 pm. "Time's ticking, and I've got about ten minutes before I'm dragged back to hell. So, I kind of need an answer."

Stacey bit her lip, and I could see the internal struggle playing out. She was beautiful like this, destroyed in such a primal way. Covered in blood and cum and drunk off her own powers. So much more willing like this.

"No more killing... by me, I mean. Unless it's absolutely necessary," she whispered.

I laughed, a deep, genuine sound. "I can handle the dirty work, but I need your soul, Stacey. It's the only way we can truly be together."

She hesitated, and I grew impatient. Reaching down, I coated my fingers in Matt's still-warm blood and shoved them into her mouth. She choked, her eyes watering as she sputtered and gagged. "Please, stop!"

I withdrew my hand, a twisted sneer on my face. "All you have to do is say yes, Stacey. It's that simple. You want this, I can see it in your eyes. Don't deny it. Don't deny yourself."

Her eyes, full of unshed tears, pleaded with me as she warred with herself.

Laughing, I reached for Matt's lifeless body, my hand coating his blood once more as I tore the knife from his chest. Stacey's eyes widened, the horror reflected there only fueling my amusement. I trailed the bloody knife down her stomach, watching her skin pebble with goose-bumps.

"What's the matter, little kitty? You want me to stop?" I asked, my tone taunting. Knowing she didn't need too much more convincing, I dipped the hand holding the knife between her legs, using the end of the handle to press onto her clit. She tried to wriggle away, but I held her hips firmly.

"Zach, please," she choked out, her voice strained.

I smirked. "Please what? Seems fear and fucking is the only way to get you to cooperate with me." I slipped the end of the smooth handle inside her, thrusting slowly as her body reacted instinctively.

"*No, stop*," she panted, her eyes screwed shut.

I leaned in close to her ear, my breath tickling her skin. "Say yes, Stacey. Give me your soul."

I pushed the hilt in further, careful not to cut myself on the blade as I held it steady in my grasp.

"I love how twisted you are. If only you could see how well your cunt wraps those swollen lips around my knife. It's so greedy. So beautiful."

She moaned and I felt her thighs clench around my wrist causing the blade to bite into my hand and her inner thighs. Stacey's eyes shot open as she looked down and saw thin cuts start to bleed through their sudden openings. I gently nudged her thighs apart and removed the knife handle from her and tossed it aside. Paying no mind to the pain in my hand, I concentrated on Stacey's cuts instead and bent my head between her legs to lap at the blood pooling out of her cuts and her head dropped back down with a groan as she writhed on the floor.

My fingers replaced the space where my knife had just been and continued with a relentless rhythm, and I felt her body beginning to respond despite her earlier protests.

"Zach," she gasped, her hands pushing at my shoulders. But her hips betrayed her, rising to meet my touch.

"Come on, Stacey. One little word is all it takes, and I'll make you feel so good. Forever. Just imagine it, pet." I quickened my pace, my thumb rubbing circles around her clit.

"No, I can't," she whispered, even as her body arched off the ground.

I chuckled, pulling my fingers away. "Seems like you're not enjoying this after all." Her eyes landed on mine, and I could see the desperation in their depths.

"Please, Zach, don't stop," she begged.

I shook my head, a mockery of disappointment. "Looks like we're at an impasse. You see, I won't finish what I started unless you say yes." I flicked her clit once, watching her body jerk in response. "So, what'll it be, Stacey? Are you ready to give in?"

Her chest heaved as she struggled for breath, her eyes glazed with desire. "I... I," she stammered, her body betraying her with each pulse of pleasure.

Reaching down, I rubbed her slowly, watching her bite her lip to stifle a moan. "You can, Stacey. I know you can." I brushed her hair away from her face, studying her conflicted expression. "It's the last step, little kitty. Just one last little choice."

She whimpered, her body tensing. "I... I need a minute."

The clock was ticking, and I let her know it. "Four minutes, Stacey. That's all we've got before this offer expires."

She opened her mouth, about to protest, so I shut her up by plunging my fingers back inside her. This time, I went in rough, pressing deep and curling my fingers to hit her G-spot. Her eyes rolled back, and her breath caught in her throat. Her walls clenched around me, begging for release.

I kept my thumb on her clit, rubbing circles while I pumped my fingers in and out. She was so close, I could feel it. But I held back, denying her that final push she needed.

"*Fuck*, please," she begged. "I'm close. Don't stop."

I chuckled, my thumb never ceasing its motion. "Say yes, Stacey. Give in."

She shook her head, but her hips rose off the ground, seeking more friction. "I can't," she panted. "It's too much."

I withdrew my hand, slick with her arousal, and trailed my fingers up her body, ghosting over her sensitive nipples. She moaned, arching her back, seeking more contact.

"You want this, Stacey," I whispered. "You want me to make you mine. Don't deny it. You've felt the magic that lives inside you. Felt me inside you. You can't turn back now. You're already mine. Say it."

Her eyes flickered open, and she met my gaze. I saw the conflict there, the internal struggle she was waging. I knew she was on the brink, both physically and emotionally. I just needed to push her a little further.

I looked down at this gorgeous little creature before me. She was soaked, a complete mess with our cum still leaking out of her cunt from before. Her body begged for release and she was about to agree to my terms, I could smell it on her. The resignation.

I slipped two fingers inside her, scissoring them to stretch her open. Her hips bucked, seeking more stimulation.

"That's it, little kitty," I purred. "You like that, don't you?"

"Yes," she moaned, her head tossing from side to side. "Please, Zach, don't stop."

"Then say it," I demanded. "Give me your soul."

I curled my fingers, finding that sweet spot within her. Her body bowed off the ground, her breath coming in short gasps. "Zach, I'm *so fucking* close. Please!"

I held her gaze as I moved down her body to suck at her clit, nibbling the bundle of nerves between my teeth. "Then give me your soul, Stacey. It's the only way."

She was sobbing again, her body shaking with the effort of holding back, and oh, how I loved making a mess of her. "I can't, it's too big of a choice."

I moved my face back between her legs and sucked on one of the cuts that was steadily dripping blood again. We locked eyes and I saw her look down to my blood-soaked mouth and she bit her lip while eliciting a moan. I held her gaze as I took it a step further and spit on her pussy, saliva and blood startling her abused flesh.

"Oh, God." She choked out, ashamed of herself for the way she fucking *loved* what I had done.

"There's no God in this, Stacey." I moved my fingers hard and fast now in tandem with sucking her clit into my mouth to worship it with the flat of my tongue. I pulled back only for a moment, my mouth still covered in blood and now with her juices. "There's just you. And me. And the devil."

1 minute left.

I sat up to leverage myself and began to fuck her with my fingers at an alarming pace with my right hand, while my left hand pressed into the bottom of her pelvis. She sat up on her elbows, looking panicked as she tried to grab my wrist and I knew I just needed one more thing...

My tongue snaked out of my mouth and I let her see it in its demon form, all pink and long and forked for her pleasure.

"Yes!" She cried out, her body convulsing as her pussy squeezed my fingers. Then, she was gushing in waves all over my hand, my forearm, and my pants that were still down around my knees.

I felt her soul surrender to mine, a delicious rush that made my own climax just minutes ago seem minuscule in comparison. She was mine now, fully and completely.

And I intended to keep her.

Stacey lay trembling beneath me, her eyes closed as she rode out the waves of her release. "It's done," she whispered, her voice hoarse from her sobs. "Take it, all of it."

I leaned down and sealed our deal with a kiss, tasting the sweetness of her surrender. "That's my girl," I murmured against her lips.

The clock in the distance started chiming and Matt's body burst into flames beside us. I grabbed Stacey close to me as she screamed and watched in horror at the show the devil was putting on for her.

"What was that?" She gasped and hugged herself to my chest as she straddled my lap on the floor and buried her head in my shoulder.

"Just the big man downstairs letting us know he accepted our terms."

Stacey shuddered and I kissed the top of her head. "This is only the beginning, little witch. Don't be scared, I've got you."

I could feel her nod against my skin and when she pulled back, the purple haze that had clung to her all evening evaporated, leaving us in the normal lighting of the room. She had a shy smile on her face, her drawn on whiskers a streaked mess from her tears and face being fucked into Matt's body and the floor.

She was magnificent.

"Now," I grinned at her and tucked some dark and red strands of hair behind her ear. "Do you still want to go to that party?"

12:01 A.M.

Epilogue
Stacey

"How's it been going with your demon daddy?" Mia snickered as she plucked an ice cube out of her cup and started to chew on it.

It had been a year since I showed up late to Mia's Halloween party with Zach in tow, and they still teased me about it every chance they got.

"*Please* stop calling him that," I begged.

"Never!" Jenna exclaimed, taking a sip of her own drink and shaking her hips suggestively to the music playing in the background. "When you introduce a new man to us looking like that, you gotta deal with the consequences and the kink names—I mean, knick names." I rolled my eyes at her before she continued, "You were glowing, girl. I've never witnessed someone look so properly fucked before. We all just about died when you guys walked in. And the fake blood? Ugh, it was such a nice touch. You both looked like little serial killers."

I laughed, feeling my cheeks flush. "I wouldn't necessarily refer to Zach as little. I mean, he's—"

"Fine as hell," Mia interrupted, winking. "Yeah, we know. We have eyes, remember?"

"And lucky for you, he only had eyes for you," Jenna added, raising her glass in a mock toast.

I smiled, thinking back to that night. It had been traumatizing and overwhelming, and I had no idea it would lead to this—me, standing in his mansion, hosting the annual Halloween party. And Matt... Well, there wasn't a body left to take care of after the flames. The police chalked it up to him being a runaway since someone had called in some bad things they'd found on his computer and my friends reassured me it was all for the best because now I had Zach. But just the knowing of what we'd done to get to this point... The thought sent a wave of nausea to my stomach, and I adjusted my cat ears, suddenly self-conscious.

"Hey, are you okay?" Mia asked, concerned. My gaze tried to focus on the shiny plastic badge of her sexy officer costume and bring myself back to the conversation. "You looked like you spaced out for a second."

"Yeah, I'm fine," I assured them, shaking off the sudden wave of emotion. "Just thinking about last year. A lot has happened since then."

"That's an understatement," Jenna said, nudging me playfully as she adjusted the stethoscope around her neck. It was pink, just like her nurse attire. Above us the candles suspended in the chandeliers flickered.

Deep breath. Focus.

"You moved in with the guy! We still can't believe you kept that from us," Mia grinned.

I bit my lip. They had no idea about the real reason I moved in with Zach—the soul-deep connection that drew us together. They only knew the surface-level story, the one that made them tease me endlessly about falling for Zach so hard and so fast. Which was more than my parents understood. I think they were just happy to see me move out of their house so they could sell it and officially move overseas where they could travel full-time. I tried to find out more about my past during that conversation and they just said they only know I was found in the woods by a hiker one morning and brought in to be adopted. I guess I'll never know who my real family is, but at least I have Zach.

"Well, what can I say?" I shrugged. "When you know, you know."

They both groaned, rolling their eyes.

"Ugh, you're impossible," Mia joked. "Fine, we'll stop teasing."

I laughed, feeling grateful for their love and support, even if they didn't know the whole truth about his past and my magic.

While they started talking about their plans for Thanksgiving, I took a moment to appreciate the deco-rations that were suspended on the high ceilings—ghosts and giant cobwebs and dozens of black and orange drapes encased the room. My magic made set-up a breeze and it had only taken ten minutes to accomplish what would have taken all day for a professional event coordinator to do. I tried not to use it all the time, but it was difficult now that I had grown comfortable using it, thanks to Zach. I loved the feeling of power that lived in my veins and if I were a better person, I guess I would feel worse about sacrificing Matt to keep them that night.

But, I *wasn't.*

I would happily take the lives of more people to keep it, too.

This room was the very room we'd consummated our little deal and now it was filled with laughter and music. At least there haven't been any other casualties since then. Well, none that I know about.

I brought my gaze back down to the crowd in front of me and spotted him across the room, his tall, dark figure cutting an unmistakable silhouette. He was dressed all in black like me again, his broad frame filling out the sleek dress pants and button down shirt, and that red skull mask—the one from last year—covering his face.

My heart skipped a beat; Zach always knew how to make an entrance.

As he made his way toward us, I felt my friends' curious gazes. They knew who he was, of course, but seeing him in that moment—so confident and mysterious—I could practically hear their own hearts beating out of their chests.

Zach reached our little circle, his mask hiding any expression but his eyes—still bright even without their demonic glow—gave me a heated stare that made my pulse pick up. Silently, he handed me a drink, his fingers brushing mine.

"I see you're still embracing the whole 'dominate the world' aesthetic." I drawled in a low voice only he could hear, my tone laced with the sarcasm he loved. He pinched my backside in response and I coughed to cover up the squeal that came with that surprise.

"Ladies," his deep voice rumbled as he addressed my friends. Jenna and Mia had been awe-struck by him all year, and it seems that the novelty of my dark beau hadn't worn off yet.

"Hey, Zach," Jenna said, her voice a pitch higher than usual as she tried to appear unbothered, but I'd known her for years.

"Looking good as always," Mia added. "Did you not have time to find some new costumes for this year?"

Zach's eyes flashed to me for a brief moment, and it was like a secret, knowing we had worn them on purpose. This was our new tradition. "Something like that," he replied smoothly, his attention already shifting back to them.

"I guess it worked out good enough last year, seeing as how you got our Stacey to finally knock one out of the park." Jenna chuckled.

Mia shoved an elbow at Jenna, her eyes wide. "Jesus, Jen."

Jenna's comment caused my face to flame with embarrassment. That night had been insane, a turning point in my life, but it wasn't something I wanted to rehash in detail with my friends. So much of it had to be left out to protect our supernatural identities.

Thankfully, Zach jumped in, sparing me from having to respond.

"Well, some things are worth repeating." Zach's voice was steady, but his eyes, searching for mine behind the skull mask, told me he understood my discomfort.

I nodded, grateful for his intervention. "Yeah, some things are."

Mia and Jenna exchanged a look, and I knew they wanted to dig deeper but instead they changed the subject.

"Speaking of repeating things, we still haven't decided on our next girls' trip. I think you've been playing house long enough." Jenna took a sip of her drink, her eyes sparkling with excitement. "Remember, Stacey, the last one we went on?"

I cringed, remembering our crazy weekend in Vegas. "How could I forget? That was the worst hangover of my life."

"We should plan something soon. Maybe a beach vacation this time," Mia suggested, her eyes lighting up at the idea.

As we dove into the details of our potential getaway, I felt Zach's eyes on me. I glanced up, catching his gaze, and he pulled the mask up slightly to smile at me before pulling it back down. It was a private moment in the middle of the party, and my heart flipped in my chest. A year ago, I never would've imagined I'd be here, planning girls' trips with my best friends while Zach—my demon—stood by my side.

The night wore on, and the party thumped around us. I talked with friends, danced to the music, and laughed until my cheeks hurt. But through it all, I felt Zach's presence, solid and unwavering. Like he was hunting me again. Every so often, our eyes would meet across the room, and a current would pass between us—an invisible thread that connected us, even in the crowd.

I guess that's what happens when someone takes your soul and vows to spend their lifetime with you.

Later, as I took a moment to myself, Zach found me on the balcony, leaning against the railing as I looked up at the black sky. He approached quietly and slipped his arms around my waist, pulling me back against his chest.

"Is it a good party?" His warm breath tickled my ear through his mask.

I smiled, leaning back into his embrace. "The best."

"I can't take my eyes off you. It's a good thing I'm wearing the mask."

The feel of his body against mine sent a jolt of want through me, and I arched my back slightly, pressing against him. Zach groaned, his hands sliding down to cup my hips. "You're being a bad kitty again," he whispered, his voice rough.

I turned my head, my lips finding his neck alongside the mask. "Am I?" I teased, my voice dropping to a husky whisper.

His hands moved boldly under my skirt, his touch sending shivers up my spine. "Stace, you're not wearing any—" His words trailed off as his fingers curled around something unexpected. His eyes widened, and a low growl escaped his throat. "You little minx. When did you—?"

I had been waiting for this moment all night, anticipating his reaction. I bit my lip, hiding a smile as I felt his curiosity and desire battle it out.

"Answer me," he demanded, his voice low and dangerous.

I straightened my back against his chest, and placed his hand over the cat tail that protruded from my skirt. "I put it in a few minutes ago. I thought you'd like it if I surprised you this Halloween. It's only fair." I purred, rubbing my backside against him suggestively.

With a sharp intake of breath, Zach spun me around to face him, his eyes scorching behind the mask, the glow of green no longer able to be contained. "We need to go to our bedroom. *Now.* Before I fuck you in front of your friends."

I shook my head, my smile turning mischievous. "That doesn't sound like such a bad idea."

Zach's eyes darkened, and he growled, "Don't tease me, witch or—"

I took a step closer, running my hands up his chest, loving the way his heart pounded beneath my fingertips. "Or what?" I murmured, my fingers lightly pinching his nipples through his shirt. "You know you want to. Take me here. Right now."

He groaned, and I saw his eyes close briefly as if he were fighting for control. But I wasn't a scaredy cat after this year with my demon. No, I craved his depraved attention just as much as he wanted to give it to me. "Goddamn it, Stacey, you know I can't deny you anything. But—"

"No buts," I whispered, raising my hand and snapping my fingers.

Suddenly, the world around us froze. The clank of glasses, the lively conversations, the laughter—all halted as if time itself had stopped. Everyone in the large room behind us on the balcony was suspended in action, their faces frozen in mid-sentence or mid-dance. The music continued to play through the speakers around the large room but that was it.

Zach's eyes widened, and he walked back into the room, a mixture of shock and awe on his face. "When did you learn this?"

I giggled, and my hands clapped in glee as I strutted across the room gesturing to the crowd that stood like statues. "I've been wanting to tell you about this one. I found it in that old grimoire you brought home for me last month. At first, I could barely get the mailman to freeze. But, I've been practicing using that technique you taught me where I channel my desire into my intentions."

"That's always been my favorite lesson."

"Mine, too." I whisper.

"You never cease to amaze me," he said, as he met me in the middle of the room. "But you do realize what this means, don't you?"

"What does it mean?"

Zach slid the mask off his face and dropped it onto the floor before pulling me into his chest. The press of our bodies together was incredible, but the heat in his eyes promised something far more intimate.

"It means, my naughty cat," he said, placing his hand on the top of my head, right between my cat ears and began pressing downwards gently until I was kneeling before him, "there's no escaping what I'm about to do to you here on display for all to see."

The taste of Zach filled my mouth, his cock throbbing, and I whimpered around him, my tongue flicking and teasing. I loved the way his piercings felt against my tongue, a unique sensation that made me so wet that he might as well have had that cock in my cunt instead of my mouth. The cold metal contrasted with his hot, hard flesh, making my knees weak and my pussy clench. I'd managed to get his pants and shoes off, but his dress shirt was still on although he was lazily working on the buttons.

Zach knew just how to drive me crazy, and he did so without mercy. His hands tangled in my hair, guiding me as he thrust eagerly, his hips moving with an urgent rhythm. I gagged, my eyes watering, and he growled above me, whispering filthy promises.

"That's it, Stacey. *Fuck*, your mouth is so perfect. Such a good girl, my slutty little witch." His voice was hoarse but he kept praising me. "Look at you. Look how good you take me. Fucking hell, I can smell how wet you are from me and it's making me even more unhinged than I already am. Do you love this? Everyone's watching us. They see you on your knees, taking my cock like the hungry kitten you are."

I moaned, my body vibrating with pleasure at his words. The idea of being watched, of putting on a show, sent me into a tailspin. I wanted to be his filthy girl, to be used and displayed. I ached to be filled, to be claimed, and I knew Zach would give me everything I wanted and more. I looked up at him and licked the tip with quick teasing flicks, swirling my tongue around the top piercing. His shirt, finally unbuttoned, was tossed to the ground beside the rest of his things.

I reached down, needing to touch myself, to ease the ache between my legs, but Zach stopped me, his hand firm on my wrist. "Not yet. I want you to ache for it, to need it so badly you can't take it anymore. To *beg* me."

His length slipped from my mouth, and he hauled me up into his arms, my legs wrapping around his waist. The feel of his thick length pressed against my stomach made me squirm, and he chuckled, a dark, wicked sound. "Patience, Stacey. I promise, it'll be worth the wait."

Then, he carried me to the grand white marble staircase in the center of the room, a spectacular backdrop for our passionate display. I couldn't help but feel powerful, being held in his arms, my magic coursing through me, ready to unleash if he wanted it, but I'd since learned to keep the visual purple of my magic inside.

Zach set me down a few steps up, and I knew what he expected without him having to ask. I bent over, bracing myself on the step, my skirt hiked up, exposing my bare ass to him.

"You like this view, don't you, demon? Go on, take what you want." I purred, my voice teasing.

"Oh, I plan to." He stepped closer, his breath hot on my skin, and his fingers trailed along my slit, making me moan. "But first, I have my own surprise for you."

I moaned as I felt his fingers curl around the butt plug tail I'd worn for him.

Zach gently tugged on the tail and I clenched around it with a low whimper. He continued playing with the toy with one hand while the other pressed two long fingers inside my other wanton flesh and I rocked back against him.

"I wish you could see yourself through my eyes," he whispered. "If you could, you'd understand how hard it is to hold back right now."

My core clenched at his words, his fingers driving into me, sending sparks of need through my body. I pushed back against him, pleading for more, desperate for the release that was teased just out of reach. And then there was something between my legs.

Wait, both his hands are on me...

What is *that?*

"Zach, please." My voice was breathless, pleading. "I need you."

He chuckled, the sound making my arousal coat his fingers and my inner thighs. "Impatient little witch. You want me to just take you, here on these stairs?"

"Yes."

All of a sudden there was a slap against my clit while his hands worked in tandem, one teasing my ass with the plug and the other playing with my pussy. I gasped as I looked down and saw the red triangular shape slap against my sensitive flesh again.

"*Holy shit.*" The words were a hiss, my breath catching as he slowly pulled the plug from my ass, making me tremble with the intense sensation before pressing it back in. "What is that? What are you doing?"

Zach growled, his voice a low rumble. "You don't play fair, Stacey. But neither do I."

Before I could ask what he meant, he lifted me without warning and set me on the stairs before he sat before me. Before I could fully straighten, he positioned me onto his lap in a straddling position. The head of his dick was pressing against my entrance, aching to be let in. He grasped my jaw in one hand and roughly turned my head to look to the side, my cat ears tumbling down the steps.

Then I saw it.

A deep crimson tail with a spaded tip a little thicker than his erection—the same thing that had just teased my clit.

He leaned into me, his mouth by my ear, hot and damp. "I told you I had something special for you tonight. It seems I can only access my demon form on Halloween now. Funny how everything has reversed, isn't it? Are you sure you want me to take you, to claim you like this?"

"Yes!" I moaned, and rubbed my wet cunt along his tip, trying to coax him inside on my own. His tail came down hard on my right ass cheek and I gripped his shoulders for balance as I cried out. He let out a dark laugh and tore my black top straight down the middle before using his clawed hands to tear my bra open so I sat in only my skirt and tatters around my chest.

Then he took pity on me, plunging deep and filling me to the core. A scream tore from my throat, a mix of pleasure and the delicious sting of stretching, having him bury himself within me to the hilt. Zach held me tight, his arms like steel bands around me as my body adjusted to both him and the plug. Finally, he began to move, his thrusts hard and deep, sending waves of ecstasy through my body. With every stroke of his cock, I could feel the tightness caused by the toy nestled tightly in my ass.

"That's it, ride my cock. Take all of it, Stacey." His lips brushed my ear, his breath hot on my skin. "You feel so fucking good, tight and wet around me. Made for me, *made for this*. This pretty cunt was destined to be fucked by a demon."

With a slow, deliberate tug, he began to pull my tail out, and I writhed, the sensation shooting straight to my center. At the same time, he used his other hand to tease my cunt, his fingers moving in a familiar, delicious circle around my clit.

I screamed as my back arched and I threw my head back, lost in the sensation of Zach pounding up and into me while his tail lapped at the entrance of my backside. My pussy tightened around him, and he grunted, thrusting harder, his hips rising off the step. I could feel his tail pushing in a little with each thrust, his piercings brushing intensely along my inner walls. My feet pressed into the step below where he sat to give me leverage as I bounced on top of him.

"I won't show you all of me this year," he murmured against my chest as his forked tongue lavished my breasts. "But I need to shove my tail inside you. I need to fuck both these holes, kitty, or I'm going to go out of my mind."

I moaned in response, not able to respond to his words. He brought the tail up to my face and I stared at it as I continued to move on top of Zach.

"Spit."

"What?" I asked, blinking, my movements stuttering.

"Spit on it."

I swallowed and nodded before leaning forward a little to allow my saliva to drip out of my mouth and onto the tip of his tail.

Zach's eyes closed and he let out a groan as it coated the spade and as I looked at it closely, it didn't look as sharp as I thought it would. No, it was thick and pulsing and fleshy. Almost like another, larger tongue.

"Such a good girl," he purred. "You're going to love this."

The gasps I let out as he pushed into my ass were from the stinging stretch, but also the feeling of having something *alive* moving inside.

Being filled to the brink was torturous in the most delicious, sinful way. Being so full on the stairs with his tail dragging in and out in a teasing dance had me moaning and writhing. Every inch of him rubbed along my velvety walls, the piercings creating sparks of pleasure that had my inner muscles clenching. My breasts bounced, eager for his mouth, needing to be touched. The sensation was overwhelming, and I could already feel the coil in my belly tightening. I was close, so close, but I wanted it to last.

"*Demon, please*. I need more." I panted, rocking back and forth.

"*Oh, fuck*, I love that," he growled in response to what I'd called him. "So needy, my little kitten." His voice was thick with lust, his cock twitching inside me. "You want my tongue back on those perfect tits? You want me to play with your nipples, pinch them, and make you scream?"

His hands gripped my breasts and he squeezed them roughly in a way that had me gushing. His tail slid back in, thick and hot, the spade pressing against the sensitive walls of my ass to rub against his pierced dick, only separated by a thin layer of skin. I cried out, the sound muffled by my hand as I tried to keep my screams in, my body trembling with the orgasm threatening to overtake me.

"I love how full I make you feel. Your tight little body is perfect for my cock, your ass greedy for my tail. I bet you wish you could keep it there forever, don't you?" His words were savage, commanding, and I whimpered, nodding my head. "Tell me, Stacey. Tell me how much you love being filled by me."

"Y-yes." My voice was a hoarse whisper. "It feels so good. Your cock, your tail, I—I need them, Zach."

"That's right, you're going to crave this now." His hips snapped up, driving into me with force. "You're mine to take, to use, to defile. This pretty cunt is mine, isn't it, Stacey?"

"Yours." I moaned, my eyes clenched shut as I rode out the waves of pleasure. "It's all yours, Zach. Take it, claim it, make me yours forever."

His fingers pinched my nipples, twisting and pulling, driving me wild. My body was on fire, every nerve ending alight with pleasure. The stairs were a blur beneath me as I moved, my senses overwhelmed by the way Zach was fucking me. The slap of flesh, the wet, slick sounds, and the musky scent of our passion filled my world and consumed me. His tail began to vibrate inside of me and I sobbed, overwhelmed by the sensation.

"I need to feel you cum, Stacey. Let me feel that sweet pussy clench around my cock." His voice was a growl, harsh and demanding. "Right fucking *now*, my filthy little witch."

I screamed, my body convulsing as I came hard around him, my pussy and muscles in my ass contracting. Zach roared, his cock throbbing as he spilled into me, his cum filling my cunt completely until it had no more room and began spurting out of me, claiming me as his own. I rode out the waves of my orgasm, my body shaking, as he continued to thrust, savoring the sweet aftershocks.

After a few quiet minutes, he slipped from my body, his cock wet and glistening, but he didn't let me go. He turned my face to his, his arms tight around my waist as he kissed me deeply, his tongue dancing with mine. I tasted myself on him, that musky, sinful flavor that made my knees weak.

I pressed a palm to his chest while I traced a skull tattoo there, a playful smile on my lips as I whispered, "You beast, you've worn me out."

Zach chuckled, his eyes gleaming with satisfaction. He nuzzled my neck, his hot breath tickling the skin there below my ear. "I much prefer when you called me a demon. Although, *'demon daddy'* I could get used to, as well."

I giggled, feeling carefree and deliciously sated. "Of *course*, you heard us talking about you. Why does that not surprise me in the least?"

He laughed and I sighed as I looked around the room at our unknowing audience. Using my magic, I conjured a soft glow that enveloped us both. Our clothes were cleaned, repaired and redressed in a shimmer of light, and the stains and smells of our passion vanished without a trace as well as my special plug. My makeup was reapplied and my hair put back into its original style, my cat ears perky once more, all as the crowd around us began to stir and chat as they un-paused. I sat beside Zach and smiled innocently at him, batted my eyelashes, and took his hand, relishing the warmth of his skin against mine.

Together, we descended the stairs, our fingers entwined. As we made our way through the room, I couldn't help the little smirk that tugged at my lips as I noticed my friends' eyes go wide at the sight of Zach's tail swinging behind him.

I'll have to explain that one later.

Outside, Zach twirled me around and we laughed and talked about the future, having made it through one whole year of madness together. It had been decided I would continue studying the craft and go on tour with Zach in the spring to search out others like me once things were finalized with his album. He wasn't just skilled at the piano, but also singing and had easily picked up the guitar the last few months which got him noticed pretty quick online.

Zach was finally getting to live out the life that he deserved, and I was getting to explore my own destiny—to be the woman and witch he knew I could be.

This demon might have caught me last year, but I was the witch who had him wrapped around her finger.

And then there was the fact that the grimoire he'd purchased at an estate sale had a way to get our souls back.

But that surprise could wait until next Halloween.

Scaredy Cat Is Available As An Audiobook

Interested in hearing these characters come to life? You can find the audiobook on Audible!

...Trust me, all the Halloween candy in the world isn't even half the treat that this audio sensation is.

About The Author

P andora Cress grew up in Atlantic City, NJ surrounded by pageant queens and stretch pants. Combining her love of horror, the macabre, an unhealthy obsession with quotes, dark romance and sarcasm, you get all the unhinged behavior in her stories. She hopes that her readers can find the passion and the humor in even the darkest of her novels, as the shadows can only be cast by the light. Pandora currently resides in Pennsylvania with her family where they spend their free time reading, browsing book stores and watching horror movies all year round.

Follow Pandora on TikTok, Threads & Instagram: @authorpandoracress. *Visit for exclusives, books and exciting updates.*

Acknowledgements

Where to even start for this one? This book was honestly just a fever dream that somehow became a tangible tale of Halloween desires. I did a very quick release for this but that didn't stop my readers from supporting me every step of the way and now we're finally here!

To my betas, you had TWO DAYS to read this and give me feedback and you all PULLED THROUGH? Honestly, the epitome of queen behavior. You don't have to do this for me, and you not only use your own time to do so but lift me up in the process - so, truly, a million times - thank you.

Dana and Zack - I'll put your aliases everywhere else but I want to acknowledge you both here personally because I didn't think I would have an audiobook done for years. Most people are unaware of how much goes into a project like that and it's an author's dream come true when their words come to life in the way you did. You both worked with me, helped me with the process and enjoyed this book as much as me and I just love you guys. I'll never forget how much fun it was getting to do this with you.

And a special thank you to @EJLEditing for always making my books look so pretty, @Ms.Morsmordre for her beautiful character art, @FromAshes.ToPages for my sexy new cover, and @TheMaskedMan96 for bringing Zach to life both on TikTok and in these pages.

9 798991 483421